# The Lake Frome Monster

If you have difficulty obtaining these
titles from your local bookshop, write
direct to Angus & Robertson Publishers at:

Unit 4, Eden Park, 31 Waterloo Road,
North Ryde, NSW, Australia 2113
or
16 Golden Square, London W1R 4BN, United Kingdom

ARTHUR W. UPFIELD

*The Lake Frome Monster*

ANGUS & ROBERTSON PUBLISHERS

ANGUS & ROBERTSON PUBLISHERS
London • Sydney • Melbourne

First published by William Heinemann Ltd in 1966
This Arkon paperback edition first published
in Australia by Angus & Robertson Publishers and
in the United Kingdom by Angus & Robertson (UK) Ltd in 1984

Copyright © 1966 by Bonaparte Holdings Pty Ltd

ISBN 0 207 14687 X

Printed in Australia by The Dominion Press – Hedges & Bell

# Contents

## Chapter One

# Death of a Traveller

The wildfowl in the trees round the lake rose in a flurry of alarm with the shot. There was a confused beating in the sky, and hundreds of wings wove a changing pattern in the early dawn. It was still too dark to see the kangaroos that bounded off into the bush and soon the silence of the vast emptiness that is Central Australia descended again east of Lake Frome.

A lone curlew gave its mournful cry but the man who was lying face down on the sand near the bore stream didn't hear it. He was dead. Beside him a billy-can drained its last drops of water into the sand and some hundreds of yards away an early-morning camp fire flickered and slowly died away without ever boiling the water which was its purpose. In fact, it was not until two days later that human feet again approached the clump of mulga trees which was his camp site.

The overseer of Quinambie Station was a practical man. When the owner of that station, Commander Joyce, sent for him on the morning of 12 June to tell him that their recent guest, Eric Maidstone, had failed

1

to arrive at Lake Frome Station and was in fact two days overdue, he had suggested that Maidstone was probably still camped at one of the two bores which he would have to pass on his way to Lake Frome. Maidstone had come to Quinambie Station late in the afternoon of 7 June and had introduced himself to Joyce as a schoolteacher on vacation. Joyce had looked curiously at his heavily loaded motor-bike, but Maidstone had explained that during vacations he combined travelling holidays with the production of articles for travel magazines. He did his own photography. He had recently been commissioned, he said, to do an article on the bore country of Central Australia and he was particularly anxious to get shots of animals watering at these bores at night. Joyce had had no hesitation in asking him to stay the night at Quinambie and when he said he wished to visit Lake Frome homestead and to photograph any bores in the vicinity as well as Lake Frome itself, the overseer had been pressed into service to tell him the route and to tell him something about the country through which he would pass.

In fact, the section of country through which Maidstone had to pass had some features which made it quite unique, not only in Australia but possibly in the world. Quinambie Station was on the eastern side of the dog-proof Fence which followed the South Australian border from Queensland to the Murray River – a distance of about 375 miles. Between the homestead and this Fence was one artesian bore known locally as

Bore Nine and almost immediately on the other side of the Fence lay its counterpart, Bore Ten. Some 50 miles farther west was Lake Frome homestead, and beyond it lay Lake Frome itself, some 15 miles away. Quinambie itself had an area of almost 100 square miles. Lake Frome homestead contained about 60 square miles, but distance in that area was not all.

The aborigines in the area told stories of a killer camel that had become a legend. Camels in general are cross-grained, bad-tempered animals, but this particular nomad had acquired for itself a reputation of being so incensed by the sight of any of the human race that it would attack without provocation. It was also said to be one of the largest camels that had ever been seen in Central Australia and, although the natives described it as 'mad fella camel', those on the western side of the Fence took care not to be caught away from their camps after sundown. While station workers on the eastern side of the Fence were inclined to pooh-pooh the stories of the animal, one of their number, half in jest, had christened it 'The Lake Frome Monster'. Dwellers on the homesteads bordering the territory over which it roamed had stories to tell of the roaring and bellowing that they had heard on their lonely cattle camps, where sounds carry for miles in the silence of the night.

After leaving Joyce, the first thing the Quinambie overseer had done was to collect two natives from the Quinambie Camp and take them with him to follow the tracks of Maidstone's motor-bike. The tracks were easy to follow to the first bore, and the natives pointed out that the motor-bike had stopped there and that Maidstone had lit a fire to make himself a cup of tea. Presumably the schoolteacher had stopped to take photographs. Beyond this bore the track grew very faint, but they followed it without much trouble to the nearest gate in the dog-proof Fence and followed it through that Fence towards the second bore. Shortly after leaving the gate, the track of the motor-bike disappeared in a churned-up mass of sand made by cattle tracks, but on approaching the bore they had seen the bike at the edge of a mulga stand. Near the bike was a camp-fire site and Maidstone's camera was hanging from the branch of a tree near the motor-bike. Between the motor-bike and the lake into which the bore ran lay Maidstone's body. The body was lying face downwards with the legs half buried in the sand blown against it by the westerly wind, which was growing stronger hour by hour ! The older of the two aborigines turned to the overseer and said:

'That fella camel knock white fella down and stamp on him.'

The overseer snorted at this and told his trackers to turn the body over. Sand was adhering to the windjacket Maidstone was wearing. The large dark stain where blood had seeped from the bullet-hole left no doubt as to how Maidstone had died.

'Camels don't carry guns,' said the overseer tersely, as he told the aborigines to get the light tarpaulin from the utility in which they had followed the tracks and to cover the body : the police would not have welcomed any more interference from crows or eagles. The overseer took his trackers back to the homestead at high speed. Shortly afterwards, the pedal radio was churning out its news to Broken Hill and the police and a retinue of black trackers descended on the site. A temporary camp was set up and the trackers put to work circling the body in ever-widening arcs to pick up the killer's tracks. They returned at dusk reporting failure, for the westerly wind had so increased in velocity that even the cattle tracks on exposed areas had been levelled out and the shifting sand had made their task impossible. Strangely enough, one tracker did report having found camel tracks through distant stands of trees and old man saltbush. He advised the police that the animal had been approaching the bore from the north and appeared to have watered at the point where the bore stream vanished into the sand and where most of its salt content would have been filtered out of the water. Other than that and a flurry of cattle tracks, nothing of any significance was found. The police made all the usual inquiries from those Fence workers and stockmen who could have been in the vicinity, but none of these inquiries nor the following inquest on Maidstone did anything to resolve the mystery of his death. His family could suggest no reason why anybody should have wanted to take his life and, after listening to what evidence the police had to put before him, the Coroner had no hesitation in finding that

Maidstone had been murdered by a person or persons unknown.

Fred Newton was in charge of the northern section of the dog-proof Fence. This section extended for 200 miles and included the Lake Frome area. To the dozen odd men who patrolled it, he was not only boss but their only consistent link with the outside world. He was a rangy man in his early fifties, and his beard was the colour of a stove brush streaked with chalk. In daylight his eyes were unusually narrowed, due to the incessant sunlight and the wind laden with sand grains. He was the type of man with whom lesser breeds never argued.

Like many of the patrol men, he used camels to transport his dunnage, and some three weeks after Maidstone's body had been found he drove his three camels to carry out his periodical inspection of the Lake Frome area. On the way north he sacked the man on the sub-section south of Quinambie, and the two of them made for the homestead where the man was paid off in time to catch the mail coach to Broken Hill. Newton was interested to see that the mail coach had brought a passenger from Broken Hill in addition to the mail and he studied him with some care.

The passenger was the physical antithesis of Newton himself. He was clean-shaven for one thing, and for another his actions were quick and his remarkably bright blue eyes had the trick of boring concentration. He was wearing ordinary go-to-town store clothes and boots, and the swag he removed from the mail car was bulky. This he lifted to a tank stand to defeat the homestead dogs, and found Fred Newton behind him.

'You are the new hand?' asked Newton slowly.

'Yes. And you must be Fred Newton. My name, *pro tem*, is Bonnay, Edward Bonnay.'

'They'll be busy with the mail and orders for the coach driver, so we'll have a drink of tea before you'll want to draw stores. The mokes are out this a'way.'

The passenger looked round at Quinambie homestead. There was the usual wide-verandahed weatherboard house, surrounded by a netted fence to keep out cattle and rabbits. Behind the homestead lay the machinery sheds, storage sheds for fodder and a number of staff huts. The mulga clump nearest to the homestead housed the kennels of many kelpies whose ambition, judging by the holes adjoining their kennels, was to bury themselves completely. No Australian who handled stock would ever part with his loyal and hardworking cattle dogs and, as on most stations, some of the dogs were living in honourable retirement and no doubt had the privilege of riding in the station utility while the younger dogs ran beside it. The whole area of the homestead looked efficient and well cared for, and the house itself had recently been painted. All this the passenger saw in a few swift glances as he and Newton walked to the rear of the homestead.

Newton's three camels and two others were lying down placidly chewing cud back of the machinery shed. They were loaded with riding and pack saddles. A short distance from them sticks had been gathered and a fire lit and flames were licking the bottom and sides of a billy filled with water. It was a brilliant day, free from dust and heat. While watching the water slowly coming to the boil, the man who had introduced himself as Edward Bonnay produced an envelope.

'Did you get the original of this official letter?' he asked, and when Newton said he'd received it the week before, tossed it into the fire.

'The Superintendent told me I would receive full co-operation,' Bonnay continued, 'and that you wouldn't talk. He also said you could arrange to put me on the section due east of the bore which is nearest to where Maidstone was murdered. I specialize in this type of crime, but usually I have to become part of the scenery to get results.'

'I take it you don't want it known you're a detective,' the overseer said in his quiet drawl. 'O.K. by me. Yes, I fixed it. The man on the section south was never much good and I just sacked him. I'm transferring to that section the bloke on this one to let you in. Know anything about camels?'

'I've had some experience,' admitted Detective-Inspector Napoleon Bonaparte, with unusual modesty. 'I suppose I shall be expected to work?'

'And how! Worst section on the entire Fence. Still, you complete your case by August, you'll escape the worst season for wind. Wind is the great enemy. How long d'you reckon you'll be on the job?'

'Could be only a week. Might be a year.'

'Oh, one of them determined guys.' Newton regarded Bony with calculating eyes. 'Well, if you don't do the work I'm expectin', I'll be putting you off. With me the Fence comes first, and murder a long way last.' He tossed a handful of tea in the tea billy, watched it tossed violently for a full minute before taking it from the fire. 'You got any ideas?'

'None. Have you?'

'No ideas to fit the facts. Bloke wasn't doing any harm to anyone. Why shoot him?' He stirred the tea leaves to make them sink, filled two tin pannikins, took from the tucker box tinned milk and a tin of sugar. 'Seems he was making for the Lake, but why go out there's a bit hard to understand. Wanted to take pictures they said. Well, there's plenty of sand and salt and mud, but you have to be patient to catch up with animals. You ever seen it?'

'No, but once I caught a killer on the middle of Lake Eyre.' Bony's mouth expanded in a grin. 'I doubt that Lake Frome is as bad. The patrol man whose section I'm to take over, what is his character?'

'Not a bad organizer as abos go. Three-quarter abo he is. He takes his wife and their children and some of the relations with him to do the work. He directs 'em. They should be getting to the base camp today. You'll be taking over two of his camels and the gear, as the mokes are used to the section.'

'And the base camp?'

'Two miles out towards the Fence and the Fence is

five from here. You come in once a month for meat and rations. Rations credited to you; meat for free. You got a rifle in your swag?'

Bony shook his head, and did not admit that he did have a revolver.

'Ought to have a gun. Never know when it'll be handy. I got a Winchester and a Savage. I'll lend you the Winchester. You'll have to buy cartridges at the store. I'm short.'

'The Savage is a fine weapon, don't you think?'

'Too right! Three-fifty yards without raising the sights. Cartridges expensive, though. They say Maidstone was shot with a Winchester forty-four. The police were interested in Winchesters.'

Bony changed the subject.

'On the Western Australian Fences section men have to keep a diary of travel and work. Is that the same here?'

'No. You done Fence work?'

'Yes. I manned a hundred-and-sixty-four-mile section in W.A.'

'Your section here is only eleven miles, and when you travel it you'll know why.'

'You wouldn't have any record of where your section men were on any given date . . . say the day the police think Maidstone was killed?'

'No, I'm sorry.'

'Where were you that day, June Ninth?'

'Sixty-odd miles down the Fence, coming north.'

'One of your patrol men, Nugget Early, was vague

about his position that day when questioned by the police,' Bony went on. 'Seems he was camped at the centre mark of his section, south of some sandhills which lay between him and the place where Maidstone was shot. The section man north of Early was at what he calls the Ten Mile, and going north. Have you anything against that?'

'Can't say I have,' replied Newton. 'By the way, Early is the fellow I'm moving to let you in. What are you getting at?'

'Both men own Winchester rifles. Maidstone was shot with one. It is of no real importance, but I like to check witnesses' statements where I can. Report has it that June Tenth and most of the succeeding day were almost windless, but so far there is no evidence whether Maidstone was killed during the day or the night. There was a late moon so it could have been done at night.'

'Why was he mooching around at night?'

'He was commissioned by a geographic magazine to take night pictures of animals drinking at watering places. There is a lot of interest in Central Australia at present. He could have been going to or returning from the bore stream at night for his purpose. What makes it hard is the absence of any possible motive for the killing. The investigating police didn't find one solitary lead although they mooched around for a fortnight. However, someone must have pulled a trigger.'

'You're sayin' it. Well, we better draw them stores.

I'll introduce you. There'll be ration bags in those saddle bags.'

With half a dozen stout calico bags, Bony drew flour, tea and sugar, as well as plug tobacco and matches. He bought a sheath knife and a box of fifty 44-calibre rifle cartridges, and all these items he took back and deposited in the saddle bags. Thereupon he and the overseer each took a sack to the station cook who gave them some forty pounds of fresh beef and a quantity of coarse salt. There was nothing further to do at Quinambie and they moved off to the base camp.

The way in which Bony helped to secure the loads and get the animals to their feet satisfied Newton that he wasn't a new chum to this work. From the neck of the last camel a suspended bell clanked rhythmically, and thus it wasn't necessary constantly to turn about to be sure the string remained unbroken. The two men walked together, the nose-line of the leading camel in the crook of Newton's elbow.

Once out of the home paddock the ground feed was more prolific, and the sparse scrub gave place to more robust growths. The way continued along a camel pad winding about low sand-dunes until eventually they saw ahead a party of aborigines. The natives were standing around four kneeling camels. The land at that point formed a narrow flat at the base of rising ground, capped with mulga, and amid the mulga was an open-fronted shed walled and roofed with cane grass.

The women about the kneeling camels were unload-

ing the riding and pack saddles, the children were
capering about them, while a man near by was sitting
on a box smoking a pipe. There were four dogs, which
came to greet the newcomers with much barking. The
man then stood and yelled at the dogs, and the children
took the camels off a little distance, hobbled them and
removed the nose-lines.

Fred Newton turned up the slope to the cane-grass
shed where the camels were 'laid' down, and this is
where the man came to them. He was cubical and
short of leg. There was no obvious mixture of the
white race in him. When he spoke there was no trace
of an accent in the voice. He was wearing dungaree
trousers, a tattered shirt and his feet were bare.

'Good-day, Boss.'

' 'Day, Nugget. How's things?' asked Newton. This
time Nugget helped to remove the loads, whereas he
had sat smoking and watching his women and children
unloading his own.

'Good-oh, Boss.' He roared with laughter and then:
'Mary got a couple of dogs coming down this time.
Aims to buy new dresses and things for the kids.'

With the ruling prices of dog scalps at two pounds
each, two would not buy many dresses and things for
the kids, but as these people set traps on the run north
quite often they would collect a scalp on the down
run.

'Nugget, this is Ed Bonnay. Ed, meet Nugget.'
Gravely they shook hands. 'Nugget, I sacked that
loafing bastard down south. I want you to take over his

13

section and get it in order. Ed will be taking over your present section.'

'Good enough,' assented Nugget without complaint, and added as though to illumine his nonchalance: 'Ed'll know what he can do with it soon as he sees Siberia.'

## Chapter Two

# Siberia

It was explained to Bony that for every Sunday the men worked they could take a day off at a favourite camp, usually in the vicinity of a bore. Accordingly, Nugget and his family would spend two days here and he and the overseer would spend one sorting out the gear and effecting any necessary repairs.

Bony was not impressed by Nugget nor deceived by his apparent cheerfulness. He was not convinced of his staple honesty, nor of his absolute freedom from bush superstitions. When it was dark he came to squat on his heels with Newton and Bony at their camp fire.

At the bottom of the slope the aborigines' fire glowed redly. It cast shadows of moving men and children across the nearer buckbush of last year's vintage, now dead and waiting only for a powerful wind to uproot it and chase it for miles. Beyond the buckbush, away deep in the dark of night, there drifted to them the musical tolling of the bells attached to feeding camels.

15

'Heard the Monster lately, Nugget?' asked Newton, carelessly.

'No, not for a couple of months, could be more.'

'Reckon there's anything in the yarn that he stamped on the schoolteacher?'

'No,' replied Nugget, disgustedly. 'The Monster ain't no camel. He's something no one's ever seen before. He's the result of a donkey mating with a wild cow, because he brays like a donkey, bellows like a cow, and covers the ground like a horse. Could have wings to him as no one's ever got close enough to shoot him.'

'But if he flies how come he don't get around this side of the Fence?'

'Wouldn't be surprised if some day he does,' Nugget predicted, gloomily. 'That stampin' on the bloke's body after knocking him down or after he was shot was put up by young Frankie. You know what Post-hole Frankie is, Boss. Has visions and things. What happened was that a loose camel come on the body and pawed it, camels being curious.' To Bony he said: 'Don't you go camping on the far side, on the South Australian side, and if you go to Bore Ten for water keep your eyes skinned all the time you're out on the plain country.'

'Isn't that where Maidstone was killed, at Bore Ten?' Bony asked.

'That's where he was killed, Ed. As I said, you don't want to be caught on open country. You keep this side of the Fence unless you're working on it.'

16

'I think it's a camel and a wild feller,' Newton said. 'Remember the time Billy the Larnikin and his camels were caught in the open by two wild camels that charged among his and created all hell before he shot one and creased the other so's he cleared out?'

Bony reflected how times had changed in the Centre. When the Afghan camel drivers lost their work to the motor trucks, they had let their animals free to roam, intending to return for them if conditions changed. However, conditions did not change and they did not return. Their camels roamed over the vast Interior to breed and become a menace. Shooting parties were organized to deal with the problem, but there were still many left deep in the desert lands.

'What part do you come from, Ed?' came the inevitable question from Nugget. The cicatrices on his face denoted tribal relationship with the Orabunna Nation.

'Queensland coast north of Brisbane,' replied Bony, without looking up from the task of rolling a cigarette. The aborigine's black eyes re-examined the stranger. Bony lit the smoke from an ember. 'I get around. Worked in all States bar Tasmania. Was spending a cheque in the Hill when I heard there was a chance of work on the Fence.'

Bony hoped this explanation would suffice, but glanced up to find Nugget's gaze passing over his clothes, his expression in the firelight hinting that the questioner would have liked to look at body cicatrices indicative of initiation. They were on Bony's back, but he was not going to oblige.

17

'What's this Siberia you mentioned?'

Nugget laughed outright, somewhat too heartily, Bony thought.

'Wait till you see it, Ed. Wait till you see Everest. The Boss calls it Everest, but it never rests. You get a windstorm and the buckbush piles against the Fence and catches the sand and raises her so that the Fence is only a coupla feet high. You lashes posts to the old ones, strings netting and wire to the proper height, and you comes back to find the next storm has took off the top of Everest and the Fence is twelve–fourteen feet high. So you get to work taking off the top you put on last time.'

'Quite a job,' Bony agreed, believing his leg was being pulled.

'Yeah, you'll say it is.'

'Don't happen often,' Newton observed, dryly. 'Anyway, Nugget and his gang will find the south section so easy they'll sleep six days of the week.'

The conversation fell into generalities concerning men and bores and local gossip. Bony smoked and listened and forgot nothing. He learned that the name of the new manager at Lake Frome was Jack Levvey. That he had only recently come to the area and had brought with him a full-blood aborigine woman who had already borne him two sons. He learned, too, that the name of the section man at the far northern end of the Fence was Looney Pete, that Looney Pete had religion, and often preached to his hat jammed on a fence post.

18

He was told that when at the top end of his section, where Three States met, Looney Pete lit a fire to boil his billy in New South Wales, tossed the tea leaves into Queensland and the meat bones or tins into South Australia. But Bony learned nothing he did not already know of the murder of Maidstone.

At ten o'clock by the Three Sisters, evenly spaced stars, the three men turned in, merely unrolling swags beside the embers of the fire. It was a cold night in mid-winter. Wakened by a movement, Bony raised his head to see Newton loading his pipe; as there was no sign of dawn, he went to sleep again. Daybreak found Bony stirring the fire embers and starting a blaze. An hour later Bony saw one of Nugget's women tossing wood on their fire, and shortly after Nugget arose and lit his pipe and warmed himself while the others worked preparing breakfast and re-rolling swags. The sun had risen when Nugget came up.

'The women and kids want to go into Quinambie for the day,' he announced. 'You won't want me, so I'll go with 'em. The mokes will want watering anyway. Anything you forgot?'

Newton said there was not. The camels were brought. A tucker box was strapped to the lead riding camel, and various packs, among which Bony suspected were the dingo scalps. All the camels were strung together, and off they went. The two women led the train, the children played games as they ran and Nugget followed after, the boss of the gang.

The morning was spent sorting out the gear. First

the riding saddle and the pack saddle belonging to the late-departed section man was looked over for repairs, and then the tools were examined. These, oddly enough, included a pitchfork and a garden rake. Then there was the baking of soda bread, or dampers, and more than half the fresh beef was sliced and salted.

Bony was now wearing go-to-work clothes of worn drill, and elastic-sided boots. His felt hat was disreputable, and had obviously been used to lift pots off the fire.

The aborigines returned just after sundown, the children tired and several of them clinging to the humps of the saddle-free camels. Bulging saddle bags carried by one of them denoted good shopping. One of the dogs limped badly and evidently had been in a fight. It seemed that a good day had been had by all.

By seven o'clock the next morning Bony and the overseer were leading their respective camels along the pad to the Fence. Bony was allotted two camels: Rosie was the leading riding animal, and Old George carried the heavier pack saddle. Soon they arrived at the Fence and turned north. The Fence, six feet high and seemingly never-ending at that point, passed over flats studded with annual saltbush presenting their blue-grey leaves to a grey-blue sky which threatened wind. Topped with two barbed wires above the netting, it looked an impressive barrier; as it was in fact.

The dog-proof Fence, as its name implies, was intended to turn back wild dogs from entering New

South Wales, as well as to halt rabbit migrations. To Bony's experienced eyes it was well maintained. The flats gave place to a long series of low, undulating sand-dunes, and there the new buckbush tinted green large areas which contained none of the old and dead weed of the previous year. The mulgas were stunted, as were the many other acacias, and they offered no protection against the westerly winds sweeping in from the desolate region of Lake Frome. Before noon they came to dense scrub and to one of Nugget's camp sites. He had put up a windbreak of tree branches and wired together poles on which to erect his tent. To the east, so that sparks would not burn the tent and gear, was the usual fireplace; a pole supported by forked sticks, and from which were slung wire hooks to carry billy-cans above the embers.

Bony noted that Newton passed this place to stop and tether his camels to trees.

Having led his camels to other trees, Bony hooshed Rosie to her knees and removed the tucker box from the front end of the iron saddle. Newton, meanwhile, had lit the fire. The billy was filled from a water-bag and whilst waiting for the water to boil, Bony said:

'I saw dog tracks an hour ago on the far side of the Fence. Nugget set his traps on the far side, I suppose, to save his own dogs being trapped.'

'That's so,' agreed Newton. The be-whiskered giant chuckled, adding: 'Never do to catch a dog this side what's supposed to be protected against dingoes. What d'you think of Nugget?'

'Usual type. Talks too much for a threequarter-caste, and that hints at craftiness. Were he and his crew called to do any tracking on the Maidstone affair?'

'Don't think so. He was camped when it happened.'

'How many windstorms have you had since it happened?'

'One. Came at the time it happened. Blew out tracks just after the blacks had done their stuff.'

'H'm! Leaves nothing for me.'

Shortly after lunch they came to Siberia. The undulating country ended at the foot of a sand range, and the Fence rose to take it like a horse at a jump. Beyond it the Fence descended to a narrow flat, then crossed it to take another hump. At the summit of this one it became evident that these ranges ran east–west and parallel, and the farther north they proceeded the higher and ever more ragged they became. The flats were bare of scrub, but the slopes carried the new buckbush, and the summits bore saltbush and wind-tormented trees. The ranges were not travellers, but permanent.

Everest had a flat top some hundred yards across. Here there were no trees. The foot of the Fence was clear of rubbish and grass. The Fence was strapped to one under it, and down on the flat they had just crossed was a stack of netting rolls and spare posts.

'Sixteen of these ranges,' said Newton. 'Job is to keep the ground clean either side of the Fence. Hoe the young buckbush and rake it away to let the sand pass through the netting, otherwise the sand is caught and she rises like magic.'

'Nugget seems to have done a good job,' commented Bony.

'His women and kids do the job. He sits on his stern and smokes. Fine life for a married man with a family. You married? Any kids?'

'One of one kind, three of the other, but I'm not bringing them here. The Number One Rabbit Fence in W.A. is a king to this. The old spinifex might cut loose, but there's no buckbush.'

'Charges the netting, piles and piles and then runs over into New South. You have to pitchfork the stuff over this side and let the wind carry it on.' Newton filled and lit his pipe, his eyes wandering to and fro along the Fence. 'I did three years on this section before I was made overseer. There ain't an inch of it I haven't done something to. I'll bet you'll have had it, time you knock off.'

Siberia! Nothing like Siberia! A living hell on earth when a storm blotted out sight and thrashed a man with buckbush, the bush of all sizes, up to four times that of a football composed of brittle filigree straw.

'When on your own you want to have a rifle with you,' advised Newton. 'Topping one of these ranges you never know what'll be on the next flat. Could be a brush turkey. It rained once and covered a flat and there were two–three million ducks on it. Another time I got two dogs. Ever seen a penentie?'

'Something of a fable, isn't it?'

'Not here it isn't. Got a jaw like a crocodile, and a body like a monarch iguana. You see one you keep wide, and if you open fire do it from opposite side of the Fence. Better not try it if the camels are on the same side. You'll lose them for sure, for they'll never stop going till they reach Sydney.'

'Quite a run, Sydney being eight hundred miles to the east,' Bony said, laughingly.

It was again up and over and down, the animals lurching up the steep sides of the ranges. Arriving at the summit of the last range, they looked down on a wide flat to a gate in the Fence.

'We'll camp here,' Newton said, at the bottom of the last slope. 'Expect you'll want to have a dekko at Bore Ten.'

They put the camels down where there was plenty of dead wood, and unloaded and off-saddled. The animals were hobbled and freed of their nose-line which ran to wooden plugs drawn through a nostril. The sacks of salted meat were slung from tree branches and then the men walked to the gate.

Scrub grew on this flat. They passed through the gateway and almost at once emerged from the scrub to see spread before them a vast naked space. There was the bore, the sunlight making a twinkling ruby of the water eternally gushing from its metal head. So clear was the air this day that they could see the steam rising from the narrow stream, and could see too the wind raising ripples on a lake of water fed by the stream.

'There she is; here against this tree Maidstone leaned his motor-bike; the camera was hooked to a bough together with his water-bag. Those stakes along there a bit marks where his body was found. Don't look like he was shot at night.'

Newton waited for a comment, but didn't get it. He watched Bony survey the immense scene and return to look closely at the camp site.

'We'll get back to camp, Ed,' Newton said, after a while. 'Sun'll be down soon, and we'll water the camels at the bore in the morning.'

*Chapter Three*

# Bony Takes a Second Look

Cattle had made the plain about Bore Ten. Cattle had eaten out the herbage, had killed the acacias, by first eating the leaves, and then scratching themselves against the dead trunks. The land was scored, and dead beasts or tree trunks were the genesis of the miniature sandhills kept to that size by the westerlies which carried excess sand on and on to begin the real hills over which passed the Fence. The bore and the lake it created appeared less than two hundred yards distant that morning even though Bony knew it was a full mile away. Brown and white marked cattle were feeding on rising ground beyond the water.

As Bony led his string of two camels after the three led by the overseer, he felt physically buoyant and completely satisfied. The air was so dry and so clean he felt pleasure in breathing it. The sand under his feet cushioned them from fatigue, and like Newton he found walking infinitely better than riding Rosie, who wasn't saddled anyway. To cap it all he was now face-to-face with the challenge of clearing up Maidstone's death. Here, where the crime was committed, must surely be something that other eyes had missed.

He drew up beside Newton when the latter halted at two stakes driven into the ground marking the place where the Quinambie overseer had found the body. There was not a trace of a track by animal or man.

'Lying face down with the head towards the east stake,' Newton said, whilst cutting tobacco from a plug for his pipe. 'Musta been making back to his camp near the gate.'

'No proof,' Bony objected. 'He could have swivelled about as he fell. He could have been going to the bore, not coming from it.'

'The police reckoned he was coming from the lake.'

'They're liable to reckon anything,' argued Bony. 'Never accept anything at face value is one of my strainer posts. We may contend which way he was walking when shot until there is proof of direction. We may promote suppositions into a thesis and waste time. The police think he was returning from the bore lake where he had gone for a billy of water to preserve the water he carried on the bike. The billy was found beside the body, emptied by his fall. That is what they think. I want proof.'

'Going to be hard,' decided Newton dryly. 'You got a job at this distance from the shooting.'

He moved off and Bony paused to follow his train, as camels always behave better when in single file. The bells tinkled, the eagles flew high in their grand circling, and Bony was happy that all was well with his investigation and the obvious fact that it was going to be hard.

Eventually coming to the bore, they stopped to watch the ceaseless flow of water pouring from the angled piping. The water dropped in a great gush into a pool of its own making and then ran away along the trench before spreading to make the lake it had also created. It had been running like that for years and would run for many years yet, although there was a slight decrease in pressure.

'Why Number Ten?' Bony asked.

'Feller that sunk it had a contract to sink ten. This was the last of his contract. It's not the official name, though.'

Again in single file they moved along the north side of the drain and then followed the edge of the lake. The sides of the drain and the edge of the lake were lined with mineral salts and a species of algae could be seen below the clear water. After about a quarter of a mile had been trodden round the lake Bony called out, and Newton stopped.

'I suppose you wouldn't remember what the weather was like when Maidstone was killed?' he shouted. Newton shook his head and shouted back:

'Could tell you when back at camp. I keep a diary.'

They went on following the lake's edge. The ground at that point was moist and presently it registered the tracks of cattle, and here Newton stopped again and turned his camels to the water. They seemed anxious not to wet their feet, and were not particularly anxious to drink. Standing beside his own two, Bony noted that Rosie was slightly disdainful, but that Old George drank heavily.

'Lower down the lake that far shore must be full six hundred yards away,' observed Bony. 'Is the water deep in the middle?'

'Only at the original extension of the channel, where it's up to your neck, accordin' to Nugget. Some of his kids tried it.'

'Shallow enough at the edge. The wind could move it into tides. Proof! Those lines of dead algae prove it. Like seaweed.'

'You don't miss much,' Newton conceded. 'Sometimes there's a lot of duck here, and swans, too. They don't get much feed, so they must come down to rest on migration flights.'

Bony would have liked to explore this artificial lake further and determined to do so when alone. He refrained from asking further questions save for confirmation of a theory. He began by saying that that stop would be good enough to fill his water-drums and that it wasn't necessary to go farther along the 'shore', and then asked:

'It would be about here that Maidstone would fill his billy, don't you think?'

'About here, yes. No need to go farther along. Water's the same anywhere on. Only makes tea.'

After the midday meal, Newton packed and went north along 'his' fence. Bony took rake and pitchfork, passed through the gateway, and worked for several hours raking leaves and twigs and hoeing buckbush out from the Fence for four feet up and over three of the monstrous sandhills. Returning to camp an hour before sundown, he hobbled and freed his camels to feed. He then started a cooking fire and later baked damper in the camp oven and boiled salted beef for the morrow.

It was the end of a perfect day. The flies were not troublesome, the air retained just a hint of freshness, and the stillness was broken only by the bell suspended from Rosie's neck. Bony felt that if such a day was multiplied indefinitely, if a man had and did live rightly, he would begin to age only when a century old. But a man seldom lives rightly, and such a day is usually over at midnight, he reflected sadly.

However, the next day was just as perfect, and Bony worked on his sandhills. The following day he took the camels to the lake for a drink, because, as Nugget had explained to him, after the fourth day without water Rosie would become cantankerous, and Old George would determinedly hobble away towards the nearest bore.

He had decided that he would circle the entire lake that day and on coming to the bore head he rounded it and proceeded to follow the eastern shore. Carrying a stick, his rifle slung from a shoulder, his eyes continuously searching, he covered half a mile. Now and then he prodded wedges of dead algae which here and there were as much as several yards from the water's edge. Thus the wind's power over this shallow sheet was proven.

Newton had referred to his diary relative to the weather on and after June Ninth. He had mentioned that wind was the great enemy of the S.A. Border Fence. Wind concerned him most, and wind was the burden Nature laid upon all his men. Wind and rain were ever Bony's concern when beginning an investigation, for on these climatic elements rested small but vital points in the search for clues in a land and under conditions where fingerprints are practically non-existent.

It was the information on wind contained within Newton's diary which made Bony decide to circle the artificial lake. From the diary the following story of the wind emerged :

June   9. Fitful breeze from the south.

June  10. Breeze from the north-east.

June  11. Entirely calm day.

June  12. Strong west wind rose late.

June  13. West wind.

June  14. Calm day.

Bony referred to his notes after he had watered the camels and filled the two five-gallon water-drums carried by Old George. During the period there had been only one day of strong wind and this blew from the west and was of sufficient strength to raise the water level of the lake along the eastern side of the lake by several inches. The position of the saline suds and the

31

dead algae proved that the eastern drift had extended in places for two yards, and again when walking along the eastern verge, Bony turned over the wedges of algae. However, he found nothing, not even water-bugs, not even the pupae of the blowfly.

Cattle tracks there were a-plenty. There were horse tracks. The tracks had been imprinted but recently, certainly after the last strong wind. He found not one item indicative of human presence in the vicinity of the lake. Not a bottle, a cork, a cigarette packet or any-thing to show that human life had visited it, until he reached the far western extremity of the lake, where he found two photographer's flash bulbs. Bony examined them closely, found they had been used, and wrapped them carefully in a handkerchief.

The bulbs gave the foundation of a story.

According to the aborigine trackers with the Quin-ambie overseer, Maidstone had made camp the day he left Quinambie, and the next morning had tramped to the lake to fill his billy with water. Why go with a small billy for water? One of the canvas bags attached to the bike was full, the other empty, and it would have been the empty bag he would have taken, not the billy-can, save as a means by which to fill the bag.

The man's camera in its leather case and suspended from a tree branch at the camp was later found by the police to contain no film. Among his equipment were two exposed films. Maidstone had taken, among others, pictures of Quinambie homestead and one of the bore head of Number Nine.

That he had gone to the Number Ten Bore lake and there had taken two night pictures was proved by the flash bulbs; but the aborigines who tracked him said nothing of this night work. They must have seen where he sat and waited for animal visitors to the lake to come within flash-bulb range of his camera. Had he returned to camp with the camera, either there would have been an entire film exposed and put away with the others, or the camera must have contained film.

Who had extracted the partially-exposed film? What had been the subjects of the pictures taken that night? The empty billy-can! What was he doing with it when shot?

The possible answers to these questions raised others even more difficult.

Bony completed the encirclement of the lake without discovering further flash bulbs, but in his mind was the picture of a man who had come to the north side carrying a camera and a billy-can filled with tea or coffee to sustain him during the night. He hoped by remaining quiet to take a picture of a dingo drinking, or a fox, possibly of cattle. He had taken two pictures, had left the lake with the camera and empty billy and had been shot when walking back to his camp. The killer had emptied the camera of film, and hung the camera from the tree branch, and the aborigines had not reported the presence of this second man whose movements must have been recorded on the sandy ground.

Maidstone had probably taken this man's picture,

and it was so important to the man to destroy pictorial proof of his presence at the lake that he murdered to effect it. Why? It was a free country. There was no question of trespass on private land. Maidstone had a legitimate reason for his visit to the lake at night. What purpose could the second man have had to feel so guilty as to commit murder?

Bony visited the camp site where Maidstone last stayed, and, without expectancy, thoroughly examined every square foot of the locality. Back at his own camp, he loaded the camels and moved off over the chain of sandhills on the southward strip of his section. There were several odd jobs to do, and it was four o'clock when he reached the place where he and Newton had boiled the billy a short distance from Nugget's camp site. It was six miles to the gate where he and the overseer had parted company, and it would be the same distance to Bore Ten.

Having hobbled the camels, he made a fire for tea and sat on the tucker box whilst sipping the tea and smoking a cigarette. The sun at late afternoon had warmth in it, but the night would be cold and clear.

The results of his visit to the bore lake were two: the one, the finding of the flash bulbs; the other the strong suspicion that the native trackers had from the start 'gone dumb'. If this suspicion were correct, then one of their tribe was concerned with the crime, and of their race was the three-quarter caste, Nugget.

It would be nothing to a man like Nugget to tramp six miles after dark to that lake, stay there for several hours and be back at his camp by daybreak. The overseer, Newton, at the time was many miles down to the south, and in any case if he did not show up at Nugget's camp by sundown it could be taken for granted he would not show up that day. Bony rose and walked to the vacated camp.

Beside the frame of poles to erect the tent when it rained, Nugget's family had built a rough lean-to windbreak broadside to the fireplace. There was litter of all kinds: paper, tins, broken toys, kangaroo-meat bones. He found also a broken box camera having a length of film trailing from it. The marks of dog teeth seemed to say that the camera had been carelessly left unguarded and one of Nugget's dogs had chewed it in play.

The film would not have fitted Maidstone's camera.

## Chapter Four

# Needle Kent

On that southward trip, Bony examined all Nugget's camping places, but found nothing of interest save a rag doll and several cartridge cases. Clearly, Nugget and his family had displayed little interest in keeping their camp sites tidy.

Bony was near the gate at the southern end of the section when Newton overtook him, and together they took their camels to a bore and then camped for the night. The conversation was of trivial matters until they settled at their camp fire after supper and smoked.

'You find anything at Number Ten?' asked the overseer, combing his whiskers with his pipe stem.

'No. You saw the camel tracks through the gateway?'

'That's so. By the way, I had a word or two about the crime with Needle Kent. He's the man north of you. Didn't tell him who you were, of course, but from what he told me I got an idea. For some time now Quinambie think they've been losing cattle. They can't find anything very definite, but on general principles they suspect Yandama's been pinching 'em.

36

Yandama is north of Quinambie and goes right up to
The Corner. Used to be Quinambie would steal
Yandama cattle and the Yandama blokes would pinch
'em back with a few more for good luck. Them was
the wild days.'

'Kind of sport?' surmised Bony.

'No fear, Ed. Dead serious. Well, Needle Kent re-
members that one night about the time of the murder
he was camped some ten miles north of the Number
Ten gate, and woke in the middle of the night to hear
a big mob of cattle passing south on the other side of
the Fence. You could say that cattle don't travel at
night, but sometimes they do without any drivin'.
Suddenly gets restless and sick of the country and shifts
themselves to another part.

'Needle's a bit of a character,' Newton went on,
and chuckled in that deep manner of a big man. 'If he
stays on the job much longer he'll end like Looney
Pete – shove his hat on a fence post and argue the toss.
He's lying under the blankets with the fire out and
he's hearing these cattle go by and reckons they must
be making for Bore Ten. They goes by, all of 'em, and
then a bit later he hears horses passing, and now and
then the clink of metal. He reckons the clinking was
being done by hobble chains round a horse's neck, and
that the horse had a rider on him. It was black as hell,
but he's sure there were several horses.'

'Rustlers?'

'Could be. Station hands don't work at night, even
them loafing bastards over to Lake Frome. The moving

cattle would be on Lake Frome country, as you'd know.'

'He didn't mention this incident to the police. And it seems he didn't mention it to anyone save yourself at your last meeting.'

'Said he wasn't going to get mixed up with cattle duffers and have himself shot like Maidstone. The point is, Ed, for your information, Maidstone could've been shot by duffers. Don't know why. He could have seen them good enough to identify them.'

Bony pinched his nether lip and admitted it was a possible motive.

'How long is Needle's section?'

'Twenty miles. Two men north of him, including Looney Pete. I mentioned this cattle business sort of casual to both of 'em, and neither said they'd seen cattle tracks passing through their gates. This would seem to make them Quinambie cattle all right. If the riders were duffers, likely enough they'd get the beasts to the Number Ten at daybreak, water them there and move 'em well away to cut out the weaners and throw a brand on 'em and take them on south.'

'Interesting,' Bony conceded. 'It will bear keeping in mind. Tell me, getting back to Nugget, what does he do with the money he earns?'

'He's got more money than me,' Newton replied. 'He's a peculiar bloke. Puts his pay cheques in the bank and writes cheques . . . thinks himself no end. You officially interested in him?'

'Only in so far as that of the Fence men he was the

nearest to Maidstone when he was shot. That is, six miles. The next nearest was the other man, Needle. Nugget seems to be generous with his women and children?'

'Never goes down to the Hill, so he can afford to. Every six months a Syrian hawker comes to Quinambie. He carries everything. So Nugget's women and kids gets dresses they wear till they fall off, and the kids are loaded up with toys and things. They are grand nights, them Hawker's Nights. What with Nugget and family, and all the other homestead blacks spending their dough on the Syrian, they have a wonderful time. I once seen Nugget smokin' cigars a foot long. Even gave me a cigar once. I was near enough to being sick.'

The overseer scrambled to his feet and filled the billy for the last pannikin of tea for the day. Bony ambled about for 'openers' or sticks to start a blaze first thing in the morning, and presently they settled down again.

'It would seem that Nugget's generosity is sometimes misplaced,' he said. 'At his central camp I saw a box camera badly damaged.'

'Nugget only cares for two things, Ed : his rifle and his camera. There was trouble at first with the camera. Mighty expensive one and Nugget couldn't work her until the Quinambie overseer gave him some lessons. Then he got to take good pictures. That box camera he musta given to one of the kids. The wrecks of toys I see often.'

Bony turned the conversation away from Nugget by asking how often Newton took his holidays, and Newton followed by putting a few discreet questions on Bony's work and home life. Then he said :

'You seem to know more about the Number Ten murder than we do.'

'I should,' agreed Bony. 'You see, I've studied the police reports, read the very few statements. You will know that the detective-sergeant and his offsider stayed at the bore for a base for over a week before the inquest. The inquest brought a solution no nearer, and accordingly I was asked to come and take a turn. As I believe I told you, I specialize in this kind of investigation in areas where there are no ordinary police facilities.'

'You think you'll nail the killer ?'

'Of course ! I always do. I've never failed yet !'

'Been at the game long ?'

'Since leaving University. Patience is my greatest asset. Once I finalized a case in a week, and one took me two years. My job is something like your Fence – it never ends. While I think of it – where does Needle draw his ration ?'

'Actually at Quinambie, but doesn't often go in to 'em. Every other Thursday he camps near the Bore Ten gate to meet the Lake Frome utility what passes through for the mail. The ute collects his list and brings it back later in the day. Let me think. Yes, he'll be at your north end next Thursday. You aim to meet him ?'

'I'd like to talk to him.'

'Good enough !'

'What's the Frome manager like ?'

'Something like Nugget, only white, that is if you could get the sunburn off him. Clean-shaven when he shaves, which is about once a week. Not like Commander Joyce, the Quinambie boss, but then his homestead ain't like the Quinambie one, either. Not much more than a permanent bush camp. Levvey don't seem to care. I was rather surprised he'd got the manager's job when I first met him.'

'The run bigger than Quinambie or not ?'

'Not quite as big. Certainly not as well supervised. Supposed to be owned by an English company.' Newton paused to light his pipe. 'Levvey gets on well with the natives, while Commander Joyce at Quinambie doesn't do so well with them. Mind you, Joyce is good with white men and he's got a good overseer under him.' Again the deep chuckle. 'Us common men don't get asked inside at Quinambie.'

'Joyce does seem to be rather aloof.'

'Too right! May be partly his wife. I don't think she likes this part of the world very much. Ah, well, I think I'll turn in.'

Bony and Newton parted at sun-up the next morning, and Bony made a mental note that the following Thursday was five days ahead. Newton told him to expect him again in a fortnight, or thereabouts.

'Be good !' he said in final parting .

So began the north trip, Bony's camels watered and

contentedly chewing their cud and rolling along like ships on a beam sea.

Bony was becoming familiar with their little ways. Neither was vicious, both accustomed to their section, and they gave little trouble until after the fourth day without watering. It was then that Rosie became restless and Old George put on an Act.

Every morning, following a drink at a bore, Old George when brought to camp would stand watching Bony. He now carried two five-gallon water-drums, which at times had to last six days. This supply had to be eked out by the man, and thus the daily average of two gallons had to meet both cooking demands and personal washing supply.

The first time Old George put on his Act charmed Bony. Bony rationed himself to three pannikins of water in a dish, and immediately he poured this amount Old George would shuffle forward in his hobbles and wait for the dish of used and soapy water to be presented to him. This he would drink avidly, toss up his head and at once bring up cud for chewing. That was what he needed, his cud to be moistened. Thereafter he could manage to get through the day. Rosie disdained such service. After her fourth day she would fidget when being saddled and loaded, sink herself low to ground so that her surcingles would not be passed under her until shallow channels were scooped with a shovel. When this was going on she would moan like a tortured soul, attempt to sink lower, flinch and generally stage a sit-down strike. In addition to the iron saddle which was divided into two compartments to take the hump, she carried the tucker box at the forward end, whilst coils of wire were hung from either side. Old George, the bullock, carried about five hundredweight of gear including the heavy pack saddle.

Australia owes an untold debt to the camel which was first imported in 1866 by Sir Thomas Elder. Camels were able to penetrate waterless regions impossible to horses except after heavy rain. It is on record that during one such expedition the animals went without water for twenty-four days. Subsequently, camels were imported in large numbers, together with their Afghan attendants who habitually ill-used them, making them cantankerous and spiteful.

A man working alone with camels has so many risks to accept that he cannot take chances, or many of them, with his camels; and so it was that the men on this Fence treated them with understanding, and it was proved that the camel when so treated was ever docile.

The men hardly ever rode the lead camel as it would be too much for the camel to be constantly brought to its knees. The rider walked with the nose-line of the riding camel looped in an arm, the nose-line of the pack animal being attached to the leader's saddle; the warning bell about the camel's neck gave instant warning if it broke away.

The constant routine of existence on the Fence suited Bony's mentality. He could think as he walked and as

he worked and as this was the most favourable time of
the year there wasn't a great deal of work to be done.
He hoed and raked and at places tossed buckbush over
into New South Wales. He found quickly the knack of
climbing over the Fence without tearing his clothes or
becoming caught in the barbed wire, and so his days
were pleasant and his nights spent in restful meditation.

Bony reached the northern end of his section at Bore
Ten gate late on the fourth day after he had parted
with the overseer. He had not been in camp more than
an hour when he saw a man approaching whom he
immediately took to be Needle Kent. The soubriquet
was obviously apt, for this man was six feet tall, as thin
as a fishing-rod, and as nervously agile as an unbroken
horse. Before Needle reached the gate, he waved both
arms and shouted:

'Day-ee, Ed! How's things? Glad to meet you.'

He crossed the road and laid his camels down near
Bony's camp.

'Black Newton was telling me about you,' he continued to shout, now without necessity. 'Said he'd put
Nugget and his mob down south. Did he tell you your
section is the worst on the Fence?'

'Something of the kind,' Bony admitted.

'Something bloody awful when she blows hard. I
know, I had a summer of it. You can have it, and
how!'

He unloaded and freed his camels in hobbles, and
on bringing his tucker box to the fire found that Bony
had made a fresh billy of tea. He spoke normally now,

very fast, his words sometimes bubbling out as they will when a man is shut off from human companionship for too long.

'Did you hear the Monster last night? Away out on Lake Frome country. I heard him just before daybreak, bellowing and roaring like he'd swallowed a blackfeller's camp fire. From what I could make out he was headed away from the Fence, which suited me all right. Heard about him, I suppose?'

'Hope he stays out that way,' Bony said, filling the other's pannikin and offering the sugar tin. 'No, I didn't hear him.'

'How you liking the job?' This from Needle.

'All right, so far.'

'Good time of the year. I've been on it too long. Got to talking to meself. Bad enough talking all day to the camels. I see you got Old George. He's a character, if ever there was one. You campin' here long?'

'I thought of camping here tomorrow,' Bony replied. 'Have to water and fill up the drums. Besides, I need to do some washing.'

'Same here. We'll do it in the morning after Levvey goes through to Quinambie. You seen him yet?'

Bony shook his head.

'Flaming character is Jack Levvey. Gets around with the abos. Brings out me stores. He'll be passing tomorrow about eight, and then we'll make for the bore.'

*Chapter Five*

# Needle and His Dates

Shortly after eight the next morning they heard a utility approaching and both went to open the gates for it. With the driver was a youngish lubra nursing a baby, and at the back were a young gin with two young children and an aborigine youth still in his teens. After the customary 'Good day-ees' Bony was introduced.

Jack Levvey was built on Nugget's lines. Although a white man, he was not much lighter in colour than Nugget himself. He was too heavy and his neck was too short for long expectancy of life, but when he spoke his voice though clipped in word-ending denoted an alert mind. His blue eyes met Bony's masked blue eyes.

'Glad to meet-cha,' he said. 'Anything you want brought out?'

'Perhaps a little fresh meat,' Bony suggested.

'Oh, we'll be bringing that. Mail, of course.'

'If there is any.'

'Too right. All right, Needle, where's your list?'

'Right here, Jack.'

Levvey checked the list. The woman beside him

unashamedly fed the baby. The children in the back were silent and solemn-eyed, and the young abo maintained his gaze upon his boots. He was wearing spurs and his clothes were flamboyant. Since leaving the showroom the utility had obviously never been cleaned. In the back beside the passengers were a few steel posts, a coil of wire and pliers and strainers – the usual mark of the station dweller who has to do his fencing repairs on the spot and often unexpectedly.

There were more 'Good day-ees' and 'See you laters' when the travellers moved on. Bony and Needle returned to the camels that had been brought in and proceeded to load the pack animals with water-drums, and tied to each towels and spare clothes. The camels were formed into a string and Bony walked with Needle. So far he had said nothing about Maidstone.

'Funny about that bloke getting shot, eh?' Needle said, jerking his head to the tree where Maidstone had last camped. 'Don't seem no object shooting him unless he happened to recognize some cove or other what didn't want to be recognized. Didn't rob him or nothing. Just shot him. You hear about it?'

'Yes, the Hill was full of it. Newton told me, too. The police talk to you?'

'They was still on the job when I come south. Parked back there. Two detectives. One of 'm a sergeant. Wanted to know where I was when the shooting was done.'

'What did you say?'

'Said I was up at the Ten Mile, and so what. He

wants to know what rifle I'm carrying and I tell him I only got one and it's a Winchester. He sparks up at that. Had I done any shooting lately? What had I shot? Mind you, this was almost a week after the murder was done, Ed, and I didn't know nothing about it. It hit me when I found the police camped just this side of the gate among the trees.'

This was substantially what the police had gathered and reported, and Bony had read. Needle had visited Bore Ten the day before it was presumed Maidstone was killed.

'Anyhow I comes south and I goes to the bore for water for me and the mokes, and later on I works here, but that must of been about two days before the bloke comes along on his bike and gets his.'

'Did you draw stores from Jack Levvey on that trip?'

'No, he tells me time before not to expect him as he's got work to do out at the lake. I don't need no stores anyway, and when I comes down again there's Jack with the police at their camp. He got stores for me that day.'

'Who told you about the murder?'

'The police, after they asked a lot of questions. Jack added a bit more when he come back from Quinambie.'

'As you said, Needle, it's certainly a funny sort of business. The police don't seem to have got anywhere.'

'Police are all right in towns, Ed. Booking you for speeding or having one too many they're real good at.

No good in this country. Why, the day before they got here it blew a bit and wiped out the tracks. The wind made me some work, too. I got buckbush same as you.'

By this time Bony and Needle had reached the bore lake. The camels took on water, and then were laid down and the drums filled. Bony said he wanted to bathe and Needle offered that while he did, he, Needle, would stand by the animals. Removing his clothes, Bony walked into the water and at fifty yards from the shore sat down with the lake up to his middle. Soaped and rinsed he came ashore feeling a new man, and Needle followed his example after Bony was dried and dressed.

At Needle's suggestion, they went back then to the bore head, where they hung various articles on the end of a long stick and held them under the gushing water.

'Not more'n half a minute for underclothes, Ed, or they'll fall to bits in no time.'

Half a minute was enough in water loaded with salt. The clothes came out almost as white as when new. They treated spare trousers to the same testing, keeping them in the gush less than one minute. Then carrying wet clothes on a forearm, they returned to camp and hung them to dry on branches.

'Washing clothes is no problem here if you're handy to a bore,' remarked Bony.

'Only thing what ain't no problem in these parts,' agreed Needle. 'What say we put on a stoo for midday dinner. I got onions and dried vegetables. You got any spuds? Have to do with salt meat as the fresh won't get here till sundown.' He rattled on: 'I always has'ta have a three-course dinner. Soup à la Bovril. Salted Boeuf. Dried Vedgies à la Mildura. Damper and bloody jam for sweets.'

'Table d'hôte,' commented Bony. 'Very sustaining, if nothing else. Yes, I've plenty of potatoes and also some tinned tomatoes we can add for colouring. Let us to work. You married?'

'Only when I goes to town. I make jolly sure I catch up on my eating, too. Usually eat at the pub or one of the cafés down Argent Street. She ain't what she used to be. The Hill, I mean. Gettin' too respectable these days.'

The men emptied the oddments for the stew into a billy, tossed in salt and pepper, added water and slung the billy over the fire. It did not matter that the meat required twice the cooking time of the tomatoes. Needle continued to give his opinions on modern town life:

'Wot mucked up the Hill, same as Adelaide almost, is the ten-o'clock closing. When the pubs were shut at six, there was always a bit of fun at night getting round the sly grog shops. Have to keep your eyes peeled for coppers in Adelaide, but not so much in the Hill. I goes down to Adelaide sometimes, and now if I asks a bloke the time or where's such a place, he gets to looking over his shoulder for a policeman. They're that suspicious.'

'Prowlers and slashers, Needle,' said Bony. 'In Sydney they tell me sleeping in the parks isn't nearly as popular as it used to be. Do you go to Adelaide often?'

'Run down when I go to the Hill. More often than not I gets the train back to the Hill the same day. No one to talk to. Different in the Hill. You can talk to anyone in the Hill.'

'The Hill is certainly more friendly, Needle,' said Bony, rolling a cigarette. 'Did the sergeant recognize you up here?'

'Too right he did. Said it was a small world and where was I on the night of June Ninth? I asked him what it had to do with him and that if I told him he wouldn't be any the flamin' wiser. So he says if I draw him a sand map he'll be overwhelmed with knowledge. So I draws him the sand map, and he still don't know if he's comin' or going. The day after he talked to me he tosses in the towel and goes back to the Hill.'

'Anyway, just where were you on June the Ninth?' Bony interjected. 'Like the bloomin' sergeant, I don't know which way I'm headed myself in this country. All this "up" the Fence and "down" the Fence. North and south would make it much easier.'

'Look!' Needle said earnestly. 'I'll tell you something to surprise you. The morning of the Ninth, I was camped across the road in the scrub a bit. That day I watered the camels and loaded up on water. That was in the morning. I got back here about tenish, and as I'm not expecting Jack to get me rations I packed up and went up – that's north to you. That night I camped at the Ten Mile, having repairs to do, and I'm

camped there when I hears the duffers going by.
Musta been two in the morning.'

'The duffers? What duffers?'

Needle spat, shrugged his narrow shoulders.

'I shouldn't of said nothing about that, Ed. I was
keeping it dark. Don't want to get mixed up in it. Anyway, a coupla days later she blew hard and I had a
deal of work to do at the Fourteen Mile, and then
when coming south again there's not much to do and I
knows I has to get back here on the Thursday to meet
Jack going to Quinambie. That's the day I meet the
sergeant instead.'

'Did you tell the sergeant about the duffers?' Bony
asked mildly.

'No fear. Tell that bastard nothing. Told Newton,
but he can keep his mouth shut. Hope you can, Ed.'

'I can be discreet.'

'Discreet! I'll have ten to one on that one. What
race is it running in? You're a rum one, Ed. Sometimes you use words like no fencer I ever knew. Yes,
they was duffers all right. Making down to Bore Ten
with a hell of a lot of beasts. Judging by the sound
could have been up to two hundred. Follerin' the Fence
they were.'

'But wouldn't they know of fencemen being camped
right beside the Fence?'

'More'n likely. But they'd also know that most
fencemen realize that cattle sometimes get on the move
at night by theirselves. It ain't unusual, Ed. I'd have
took no notice at all if it hadn't been for the clinking of

hobble chains slung from a horse's neck. Same as them now on the camels.'

The animals were lying down. Habitually, when not in use, the two sets of hobbles are strapped together and then strapped to the leading camel's neck.

'Them hobbles was around the back of à pack-horse or a spare going down with the riders. It was that dark I couldn't see, and I wasn't going to rush to the Fence and sing out a goodnight. Leave 'em to it, I says, they weren't my cattle.'

'And that was very early on June the Tenth?'

''Bout two in the morning. Could be guessin', though. As I says, it was a dark night. No stars out. Nothing.'

'No watch?'

'Couldn't be bothered lookin' at it,' replied Needle. 'No cause for it. Nothing to do with me if all the Quinambie cattle is pinched. I'm keeping out of it, as I tells Newton and now you. And you take a tip, Ed: what the flamin' eyes don't see, the heart don't do no grievin' about.'

'Were the cattle moving fast?' Bony pressed.

'They were moving all right. I reckon they were aimed to get at the bore lake before daybreak. No chance of anyone being around at that time. It was too early for Jack or his boys, and too early for a Fence man to be going for water. Yes, they'd get 'em to water before daybreak and then drive 'em down to the south-east to get 'em away from the Fence by daylight.'

'You are sure of your dates?'

'Too right!'

'Then they would have passed this gate and crossed the track beyond it, eighteen hours after Maidstone got here from Quinambie?'

'That's the way I worked 'er out, Ed.'

'You don't think the duffers could have anything to do with the murder, eh?'

'I don't reckon so,' said Needle. 'All they wanted was to get the cattle as far away as possible. No flamin' duffer in his right senses would bring the sergeant out here looking for someone who done a murder. On their way past Bore Ten they wouldn't even see Maidstone's body in the dark. I reckon he'd been dead a long time by then.'

'Then we can forget about the duffing.'

'Too right!' There was a note of relief in Needle's voice. 'That stoo's beginning to smell good. Should be done soon.'

With the final addition of flour to thicken it, the stew was quite a success, and after the meal they fitted the camels in their hobbles and again relaxed to gossip. When Needle mentioned Nugget and his family, Bony bluntly asked Needle his opinion of them. Needle's opinion was not good.

'Nugget, Ed, ain't my billy of stoo. He's a know-all. Talks too much to Newton and the Quinambie people. The police was right in his alley, so I was told. Hung around 'em when any respectable bloke would've cleared out and left 'em to their jobs. He was camped, so he says, midway along his section the time of the murder, and he got to his top end, that's this gate, the day after the police got here. Hung around two–three days. Did a bit of trackin', him and his lubras, but the wind blew out that job.'

'Did you meet him here often, like we met?'

'No, oh no! Not often. It's months back since we happened to collide sort-of. As I said I haven't got any time for him. Throws his money about like he thinks the bosses do. Reckons he's a bit above the blacks because he runs a job. Runs it is true. Sits on his stern and makes the lubras and kids do all the work. It's why Newton kept him on your section. Newton didn't do you no favour by putting him off it and you on it.'

'How d'you get on with Newton?'

'Good-oh! As long as you satisfies him with your work he's pretty easy. If you falls down on it he goes to market. It's his Fence and don't you forget it.'

'He gave me that impression.'

'And another thing, Ed. If you can do the managers a favour, you know, report anything wrong or holding up their cattle, you do it, rememberin' that you gets free meat. No harm keepin' on the right side of 'em.'

'What about the duffing incident?' countered Bony.

'That's different. They runs their cattle, I run my section.' Needle looked annoyed. 'I'm only a labouring cove, see. What happens to their cattle wholesale like, is not our business. What I means is, let's say, a beast gets caught in the Fence or had fallen into a bore channel. Well, do a little getting it straightened out. And if you are asked what the country's like in some place or other – you know what I mean.'

'Yes, I think I do,' Bony admitted, without smiling.

## Chapter Six

# Bony Visits Quinambie

When he had once again reached that point of the Fence nearest to the Quinambie homestead, Bony decided to interview Commander Joyce. He knew that this visit would not coincide with the monthly one permitted to purchase stores and obtain meat, and he was also aware that this visit could cause comment. Accordingly, he turned off the Fence and camped the night at Overseer Newton's cane-grass shed.

The next morning he put his camels down behind the blacksmith's shop, watered them shortly after nine o'clock and then called on the cook. The cook was large and placid, with a few darkish strands of hair plastered as if glued over an otherwise bald head. His Cockney origin was at once betrayed by his accent.

'Cor blimey! What's wrong with you, Ed?'

'Got the gripes bad,' Bony replied. 'Not used to that bore water, I expect. Been giving me hell. Have you any chlorodyne?'

'I have so. Wait a mo'. I'll give you a snort.'

'Fifteen to twenty drops is the correct dose, I think,' Bony cautiously advised.

'That's what it says, Ed. I always play fair.' Bony grinned.

'Well, not always,' the cook admitted. 'I got a drunk hoisted on me once. He was getting well into the horrors and was a ruddy pest. I give him half a bottle and blow me down if the bastard didn't turn blue. Had to walk him around all night, but by hell he was sober in the morning.'

'A pleasant experience, but a relief,' commented Bony, drinking the proper medicinal dosage. 'Boss at home?'

'Over in the office. You take some chlorodyne out with you. I'm never without it. Have a drink of tea?'

'I'll see the boss first, Harry. That stuff's easing me stomach already. Giving it a bit of warmth. See you later.'

Commander Joyce probably never knew he was referred to by his wartime rank. Verging on seventy, he was sparse of frame but still upright and nimble on his feet. He sat that morning behind a desk stacked with papers and account books. It quickly became clear that he was without a book-keeper, although it was normal for a station of Quinambie's size to have one. Looking up, he saw Bony in the doorway.

'Hullo! What do you want?'

His voice was mellow, his gaze direct. Bony met the deep-set dark eyes and advanced.

'I am, *pro tem*, a Fence worker. I have here a letter from the Divisional Police Superintendent at Broken

Hill which will in part explain my presence. I am also in need of chlorodyne.'

Commander Joyce opened the foolscap envelope, began to read, hesitated and invited Bony to be seated. Having read the request to assist Detective-Inspector Bonaparte in any way possible, he pursed his lips, took up his pipe and lit it. He looked at Bony quizzically.

'The name is Ed Bonnay.'

'Very well. What can I do for you?'

'Give me some information, if you will,' Bony said and lit a cigarette. 'Is there the possibility of being overheard? May I close the door?'

'Better. Someone could come along with my morning tea. I am not sorry to get away from these cursed returns for a while. All these stock schedules make me tired. You are on the Maidstone affair, I assume?'

'Yes,' answered Bony, returning from closing the door. 'It's the kind of case they saddle me with when normal police investigation gets bogged down. Usually something in the wide-open spaces.'

'Well,' said Joyce dryly, 'these are certainly wide enough for you. However, it must be interesting work. Are you actually an Inspector?'

'Yes, I rose to that rank, but not without some hindrance and difficulties. I have kept the rank because I have been fortunate enough never to fail on an assignment of this kind. I hope this isn't the one that must come along soon. Since working on the Fence I've talked to the man Nugget, Needle Kent, and of course Newton. You will know the type of men they are and will agree with me that they have to be handled with kid gloves. Bluff and bullying will merely erect a brick wall of silence. That's why I am working under an alias and must continue to do so for some time to come. I hope you will respect the alias.'

'Surely. Anything I can do, call on me – er, Ed.' Joyce smiled a trifle grimly.

'Thank you. Since you have been managing Quinambie have you ever been worried by loss of stock?'

'To be quite frank, Ed, I don't know. My predecessor had that kind of trouble. It used to be very bad early this century. This really isn't my line of country, you know. But I've had the feeling lately that all isn't well. That is one reason I'm ploughing through these stock returns.'

'I've been informed that early in the morning of June the Tenth a large number of cattle were driven down the Fence on the west side and were heard by Needle Kent. He estimates the time at two o'clock when they passed his camp.'

'The devil! Is Needle sure?'

'Speaks with conviction. Says the night was very dark and his camp fire was out. He couldn't see anything, but he did hear the cattle and, later, hobble chains clanking from a horse's neck.'

'Never said anything to me about it. Nor do I think he did when he was questioned by the police.'

'He has an aversion to becoming mixed up with it,' Bony explained. 'While I think it improbable that it touches my investigation, I have mentioned this business in my report to the Superintendent and doubtless he will have some extensive inquiries made farther south as to whether cattle are being disposed of. For that reason I would rather you did not mention it to Levvey or to anyone else. Agreed?'

Joyce nodded, his eyes gleaming as though he wished that he were Drake and the rustlers were on his quarter deck.

'June Tenth?' he said.

'Very early on that day. It was on the Eighth that Maidstone left you to go to Lake Frome Station. Your overseer found his body on the Twelfth, remember? Did he notice significant cattle tracks crossing the path beyond the gate?'

'Didn't mention it if he did.'

'He had two blackfellows with him, I understand.'

'True enough,' agreed Joyce. 'He drove a utility. They rode in the back. They pop out to open and close the gates, of course.'

Bony knew that the overseer would be an excellent judge of cattle and their ways, and that behind this duffing business there was the accepted submission that cattle will sometimes move grazing ground at night. A bushman on seeing the tracks of stock crossing a road or following the Fence would think they were travelling freely unless he happened to see the tracks of following horses.

'Tell me something about Maidstone,' asked Bony at this juncture. 'How did he appeal to you?'

'Oh, a nice kind of chap,' was Joyce's verdict.

Showed us some of his finished pictures and overhauled his gear. Intelligent, too. Quite a good talker. Bit of a shock finding him dead.'

'Can you recall when you first mentioned him to the people at Lake Frome?'

'It would be the evening before he left. I spoke to Levvey on the transceiver and I told him about Maidstone and his intention to arrive there the next day.'

'Levvey is friendly with the aborigines, I'm told.'

'He is, but he seems an intelligent fellow. His woman makes a good wife, by all accounts. Not that I can approve. Still, Levvey is the type of white man with no background other than horses and cattle, no culture.'

'You have a radio routine, I suppose?'

'Yes, we both used to go on to the air at nine of an evening. Just gossip, you know. When I was away my wife used to take over. Lake Frome is our nearest neighbour. The last manager and his wife were more our cup of tea. Even had the odd game of bridge. Since Levvey arrived, the radio is mainly used for messages and any matters of joint interest relating to weather or stock.'

'Please pardon me for troubling you further,' Bony said, rolling another of his atrocious cigarettes which were pointed at both ends, 'but would you mind if I talked to your overseer?'

'Not at all,' said Joyce. 'I think you'll find him at the machinery shed. He is getting the tractor overhauled.'

Bony introduced himself to the overseer only as Ed Bonnay and drew him out of earshot of the mechanic working on the tractor.

'Your boss said I could talk to you about finding Maidstone. I have a personal interest in the case, and your boss knows why. He also knows that I want you to forget I've been asking questions. That good enough for you?'

The overseer looked at him and suddenly grinned. 'O.K. Ed,' he said. 'If it's O.K. with the boss, I haven't seen you today. Just what do you want to know?'

'Cast your mind back to that day you found Maidstone. With your two aborigines you arrived at the gate, passed through it, and being familiar with the track to Lake Frome, continued until you saw the motor-bike against the tree. What happened then?'

'What happened! Why, I looked towards the bore and saw the crows worrying something and one of the blacks said it looked like a man. It was, too. Maidstone was lying face-downward, and his billy-can was lying within a few feet of the body. When we reached it we saw the camel pads and then we had all this nonsense about the Frome Monster. One said the Frome Monster had stamped the visitor to death, the other, the older, said not. So we turned him over and discovered the blood staining the sand.

'After that I told the abos to circle for tracks, and I sent back to the utility for the tarpaulin, which we placed over the body. The abos tracked as far as the bore lake and the bore itself. And then, I drove like hell back to Quinambie to report.'

'Did your aborigines seem uneasy?' Bony pressed.

'Only on account of the Monster. Seems they didn't like being in the open on the west side of the Fence. Same with the Frome blacks. As Levvey told me, they don't mind scouting around on horseback, but they hate to work on foot.'

'They did not find any significant tracks?'

'Not that day. The next day it blew hard and ruined any chance of finding anything.'

'That was the day the police arrived?'

'That's so. A sergeant and two constables in plain clothes. One of the constables took the body down to the Hill, and I fixed the others with a tent and camping gear. They made Maidstone's camp their headquarters. It's the most devilishly funny business I've ever come in contact with.'

'Well, I'm obliged to you,' Bony said getting to his feet. They had been squatting in the shade of a giant coolibah beside the shed. Returning to the homestead, Bony again sought out Joyce.

'Well,' he said, 'I found the overseer, thanks. You might impress on him not to mention my curiosity.

'I'd better be on my way back to the Fence. I came in for chlorodyne as the excuse, and I'd like you to sell me a bottle which, after all, I may need. And here are some letters I'd like mailed. One of them, as I mentioned, is for the Superintendent. He'll do what he can about the duffers – if there were any.'

'Good. I'll do that.' Commander Joyce hesitated. 'Sorry about the alias. Otherwise the wife and I would be happy to ask you to stay with us.'

'Nice of you, but I have some buckbush to remove from Overseer Newton's Fence.'

The chlorodyne was procured from the store and Bony sauntered to the kitchen detached from the house. The cook met him with the questioning grin.

'How did you find the old bloke?' he wished to know.

'Quite chatty,' answered Bony. 'How was the water at Bore Nine and things like that. I bought the chlorodyne. Have another dose when back in camp. You mentioned a cup of tea?'

'I did. I made it just now. Take a pew while I pour her out. Bit of brownie in the cake tin. You liking your job?'

'All right, so far. I'm told it's rough when it blows.'

'So they say, Ed. Never seen the Fence. Never want to. You heard the Monster yet?'

'No. I doubt if there is such a thing.'

'Well, both Nugget and Needle Kent heard it more'n once. The blacks are scared of it. Old King Moses told his people to keep well wide of the Fence, and not to go wandering around at night.'

'He the abo boss?'

'Yes. And really bosses too.'

'And is he the Medicine Man?'

'No. Charlie the Nut's the Medicine Man. They say

he points the bones and things. Not that I believe he can do any harm with 'em. Lot of mumbo-jumbo in my opinion. Cor blimey, if they could blast a man with a bone, things would be crook!'

'Where are they camped?'

'Got their permanent camp out at Bore Six. Boss won't have 'em in here 'cept Hawker's Nights. Have another cuppa.'

'Thanks, I will. My stomach feels better already. Will you be able to spare me a bit of meat?'

'Plenty. You better take a loaf of yeast bread. Better than damper. Wonder any man's stomach stands up to much damper.'

'Decent of you. How many hands have you to cook for?'

'Three whites and a couple of blacks. Then there's the boss and his wife, a book-keeper when there is one, and visitors. Not a bad job; me wife looks after the main house.'

'One thing, the wages mount up. Go outside often?'

'Every year for six weeks.'

Two men came in, greeted the cook cheerfully, nodded to Bony, helped themselves to the teapot and the brownie cake. They were introduced to Bony as the carpenter and the mechanic, the latter being a slight man in khaki overalls. He wanted to know if Bony had heard anything about Lake Eyre being chosen for an attempt on the land speed record, and Bony said that he had heard rumours in the Hill, but nothing was definite as far as he knew.

'How's me old pal, Needle, coming along?' asked the carpenter. 'Seen him yet?'

'Yes, we were camped together at Bore Ten several days ago,' Bony replied. 'As his nickname implies, he is a bit thin.'

'If he was any thinner he'd be blown away in a storm,' said the cook. 'Biggest liar in the back country. Thinks 'em up when he's workin'. Nothing else to do.'

'Like that Monster yarn of his,' agreed the carpenter, and to this the mechanic took exception, saying there was something in it.

'Told me the Monster was roaring around him in the middle of the night,' the carpenter volunteered. 'Told me another time five horsemen rode past him and not a one said a single word. He's getting like Looney Pete. Time he came off the Fence and took a job in town. How long's he been on it?'

The overseer said it was six years, with a break to town every year, and agreed that Needle Kent would soon go 'wonky' if he didn't look out.

Bony left soon after this discussion, glad of the fresh meat and the loaf of bread given by the cook. He wondered often if Needle's story about the duffers was not a pack of lies.

*Chapter Seven*

# A King and His Offsider

A few days after his interviews with Commander Joyce and his overseer, Bony had his first experience with the buckbush. The whitish sky predicted the wind hours before it rose. It first came from the north-west and then veered to the west with ever-increasing force. Bony had been feeling pleased with his section, the ground at the foot of the Fence being clear of weed and debris from the top end to the bottom.

First the wind took off the old leaves from the gums and teased the acacias, glueing them to the netting, and then prodded the dead buckbush until it broke the filigree balls from their stems and rolled them over the ground to the Fence. Soon they became a mile-wide procession, charging the netting, smashing themselves against it, becoming the foundation of a growing wall of yellow lace.

Bony was on the undulating country south of the sand ranges, and with the pitchfork worked to toss the buckbush over the Fence into New South Wales, where the wind carried it away. It was a losing battle, for as he moved forward the bush was plastered against

the Fence behind him, and eventually he surrendered
to the wind and took his camels to the shelter of a
stand of cabbage trees. There he removed the loads
and freed them in hobbles, but they promptly lay
down with their rumps to the wind.

Along the lee-side of the Fence herbal rubbish remained undisturbed, but the air was filled with flying
red dust and the sun itself turned red. It was as though
this western strip of New South Wales were below the
lip of an endless dam. Hour after hour the buckbush
came flying past Bony and when he looked towards
the Fence he could see nothing but the yellow wall
over which sailed the bush in large tangled masses,
some of it to blast his tree, and some the rumps of the
kneeling animals. It continued to blow the remainder
of the day and well into the night.

Towards morning the wind died away and the
camel bell denoted that the animals were up and feeding. At break of day Bony rolled out from under a
tarpaulin laden with sand, built a fire and boiled water
for tea.

To westward, what at first appeared as a dark
sand range emerged as a gigantic wave of grass, and
all the work Nugget and he had done was now un-
done.

All day he forked buckbush over into New South
Wales. The next day he had to take his camels to
water and on returning he raked up the debris into
heaps and burned it. When Overseer Newton came
along he had cleaned the Fence for two miles.

'How you liking the job?' asked the be-whiskered man, his dark brown eyes gleaming with humour.

'I don't think I'm going to like it,' was Bony's verdict.

'What's the Fence like farther south of my section?'

'Not too bad down there. This'll be about the worst. Of course, Everest could be buried or have its summit blown off. How are your mokes for water?'

'They filled up the day before yesterday.'

'Then I'll camp the night with you.'

At sundown, Bony ceased work and joined Newton who was baking a damper loaf, and together they boiled salted meat for the morrow and dined on cold meat and potatoes. They talked of the alleged duffing and Newton said that if there had been any duffing the stolen beef had not passed through any gateway on his length of Fence.

'I thought I had better report it to my Superintendent, and as there were some matters I wished to talk over with Joyce, I went to the homestead the other day with the excuse of an upset tummy. Told him who I was and he co-operated well enough. So did his overseer – I had to take a chance there. There is one point I missed. The name of one of the abos who accompanied the overseer when he found the body was Posthole Frankie. D'you know who the other man was?'

'Yes, Charlie the Nut.'

'Charlie the Nut is the local Medicine Man?'

'You've said it, Ed.'

'I also heard from one of the hands that Needle

Kent is given to romancing. D'you think this yarn
about the cattle rustling was imagination?'

'Could be. Needle does imagine things. I'm not
going to say he deliberately lies, but he should take a
spell from the Fence and get away down to the Hill.
He doesn't even go to Quinambie for his rations and
sees no one bar me for months at a time.'

'I arranged to meet him at the top end. Spent a day
with him.' Bony lifted the lid of his camp oven to
inspect the baking damper. 'Needle could have been
mistaken about the dates of that movement of cattle.
He could have fancied he heard hobble chains clinking. He was adamant that he would not report the
incident and he advised me not to take notice of what
he inferred was a slip of the tongue when mentioning
it.'

'Well, I don't take much notice of him,' Newton
said. 'He's somewhat unreliable even when telling me
about his work and what not. The only thing in his
favour about the cattle is that there were cattle tracks
across the road when Joyce went out to look for Maidstone. But that doesn't necessarily mean the cattle were
being driven.'

'Joyce was not sure if any duffing was going on at
the moment. Needle told me there was now and then.'

'Sooner believe Joyce.'

'This Charlie the Nut,' Bony veered, 'what kind of a
character is he?'

'Run of the mill. Works for Quinambie when they're
busy with the cattle. Loafs otherwise.'

'Keeps his fellow abos in order, I suppose.'

'Does that, Ed. The mob around here ain't advanced much. Pretty isolated. They has their ceremonies out at Bore Six, has a fight now and then, but no one troubles about them. There was a couple of killings ten or twelve years ago, and the police had to smooth 'em out, but didn't get far with 'em.'

'None arrested for the killings?'

'One arrested for one of them. A buck got three years. They been good ever since.'

'The Medicine Man – young or old?'

'I'd say would be about fifty. Chief Moses would be a hundred and fifty and never a wash in his life. Keep to windward of him if ever you meet him. Before the Monster turned up they'd joined with Lake Frome abos and went walkabout out there. It seems that when the Fence was built it sort of divided the tribe, and them in South Australia elected their own chief. You know much about the abos?'

'Very little,' lied Bony. 'Haven't had much time to study them. I was brought up in a mission and went to University later on in Brisbane.'

The conversation drifted into generalities, and the next day Newton pulled away for the north and Bony returned to his work. In mid-afternoon he had a visitor; in fact, two.

They came along the Fence from the north and he did not see them for the wall of buckbush ahead until a horse appeared with a small ancient astride it, and a young buck on foot.

'Good day-ee!' greeted Bony, who now dropped the fork and began the manufacture of an alleged cigarette. The horseman reined the animal to confront Bony through the wire. The pedestrian followed. He was rather a good-looking aborigine.

'*Gibbit tobacco*,' ordered the ancient, and Bony thoughtfully passed a pinch through the netting.

'Old Moses can't talk English,' volunteered the young man. 'Can you spare me a cigarette?'

Bony passed the second pinch of tobacco and a paper. They had matches, and the young man said:

'Lookin' for a horse. You seen any tracks down south?'

'No. What's your name?'

'I'm Posthole Frankie. Takin' a spell from Quinambie. Heard about you. You're Ed Bonnay.'

Moses muttered something and Posthole Frankie grinned and translated.

'Moses wants to know if you heard the Monster lately?'

'No, I haven't heard him at all.'

'Seen his tracks about?' Frankie asked.

Bony shook his head. 'Wouldn't recognize them if I did. What is he like?'

'Wouldn't know.'

The youth spoke to Chief Moses and the ancient muttered, chewed the tobacco for a space, muttered again and pointed at Bony.

'The old bloke wants to know where you come from,' said Frankie irreverently.

Bony gravely removed his shirt and then the under-vest, turned about to permit Moses to see the initiation cuts on his back. Putting on his vest and shirt he asked Posthole Frankie if Chief Moses was any the wiser.

The inquiry being translated, the Chief vigorously shook his hoary head and asked for more tobacco. Bony said he was short, Moses then produced a fine tobacco plug, gave it to his escort to slice a chew as he had no teeth.

'Cunning feller,' observed Bony. 'Tell him I come from North Queensland, not that he'll know where it is.'

Without warning, the Chief reined off the Fence and he and Posthole Frankie departed in a north-easterly direction. A pleasant interlude, thought Bony, maybe not without significance, and fell to working.

At sundown he went for his camels and found they had roamed a mile away. He brought them back to camp and gave Old George his washing water to tide him till the next morning, as George was heading for a bore when caught up with. It was two days later on that he took them to Bore Nine, this bore being the closest to his work.

The bore lake was not as large as that at Bore Ten. He tied the camels down by passing a line about their angled forelegs and then circled the lake. There were no cattle tracks and not a single horse track. Now, Chief Moses had come from this direction and had left roughly in the direction for Bore Nine, yet neither he nor Posthole Frankie had circled the lake to find if the missing horse had called here for a drink. Doubt was thus cast on the missing horse story, and that meant Chief Moses had a different objective. Bony wondered if the true reason for the trip was to scrutinize him.

The recent windstorm had wiped clean this page of the Book of the Bush, and Bony found nothing significant of Maidstone's halt. Tenaciously, he made a second encirclement, this time along the fringe of the encircling scrub, a journey of about two miles at the edge of the open space created by the cattle.

The road taken by Maidstone touched this fringe opposite the bore head, and here he did find an empty matchbox partly buried by sand and lying at the foot of a tree. It could have been discarded by Maidstone when he stopped here to photograph the bore, or it could have been thrown away by the overseer or one of his two offsiders. There was no trace of a fire to boil water. Had Maidstone stayed a while for a meal, the sand would now cover the embers.

Governed by habit, Bony pocketed the matchbox. The brand was not the same as that he had purchased at the Quinambie store, and doubtless had been discarded by Maidstone.

The overseer had told the police that Maidstone had lit a fire to make noonday tea. He had seen the ashes of that fire. Now the wind had buried the ashes with sand Bony felt he should check. Accordingly, he brought the rake and began to rake the ground all

75

about, giving special attention to the small sand hummocks. He unearthed tree debris and eventually brought to light the residue of Maidstone's fire. There were the streaks of burned sand, the ash having been carried away. There were the ends of sticks and the unburned ends of thick boughs. It had been quite a large fire, much too large merely to boil water in a billy-can.

Here was a discovery that posed many questions. The embers proved the size and the time of the burning, and this in turn strongly indicated that the fire had burned all night.

It had been thought all along that Maidstone had stopped at this bore to photograph it the day he had left Quinambie, had boiled water for lunch and then gone on to Bore Ten. If he had camped here the day he left Quinambie, then he would not reach Bore Ten until the Ninth of the month, not the Eighth.

Bony thought back to the information given by Needle Kent concerning the travelling stock. Needle had said that he was camped at the two-mile north of the gate and heard the passing cattle about two o'clock on the morning of the Tenth. This would have put the rustlers and the cattle at Bore Ten early in the day on which Maidstone arrived there – not, as it appeared from the police reports, in combination with Kent's evidence, twenty-four hours after Maidstone's death!

In this case, it was possible that the rustlers could have had something to do with the shooting of Maidstone, but the absence of motive made it highly improbable. It still seemed likely that the rustlers had left Bore Ten before Maidstone arrived, although the margin of time had become much less.

The size of the fire embers could well have deceived the overseer but would not have deceived the two aborigines with him. The question that concerned Bony was why they had not pointed out to their boss that Maidstone had almost certainly camped here on the night of June Eighth? Perhaps, it had been due to laziness. Perhaps, they had not been consulted by the overseer, who had taken it for granted that Maidstone would have made more mileage than this camp fire showed and had actually been at Bore Ten on the Eighth.

Bony raked the sand over the embers and then removed the marks of the rake everywhere with a leafy branch, as well as his own tracks about the fire site. When on his way back to the Fence, he became convinced that the aborigines had 'gone dumb'. They knew something vital about the murder and had been instructed not to co-operate with either the overseer or the police.

## Chapter Eight

# Broadcasting Sly Hints

If the aborigines were his opponents in this Maidstone investigation, then Bony knew he was up against a wily and cunning foe. It would not be the first occasion when he had found himself opposed to a black rather than a white enemy of the law. If the theory was – for as yet it was only a theory – that the station aborigines knew who had killed Maidstone, then the lack of success of the police could be explained.

The subject occupied Bony's mind as he continued to labour to clean his section of the Fence. The weather had returned to clear calm days and cold nights when a camp fire was a comfort and lifted the roof of stars to an unimaginable height. Sometimes he wondered how men could stand this kind of work and the harsh conditions governing it. True, the pay was good, there was no clock or time check, and freedom of movement was absolute. The type of man who chose to work on this and other Government Fences would not be tortured by a factory siren, while the office worker condemned to labour on a Fence would become mentally unbalanced much more quickly than Needle Kent.

Eight days after talking with King Moses and his offsider, Bony saw Newton and his camels coming down a long slope. During the interval he hadn't seen as much as a dingo, and he was very glad to see the forthright overseer.

'How's things?' was Newton's greeting.

'The Fence isn't as good as when Nugget's crew left it.'

'Many hands make light work of it, Ed. You haven't done so bad. Mount Everest didn't get a beating this last time. How are you on rations?'

'I'm out of potatoes and I haven't had fresh meat for a fortnight. I was going into Quinambie when I get down to the turn off to your shed.'

'We can go in together. The Fence will hold up for a day or two. Anything happened? You find out anything?'

'Had a visit from old Moses and Posthole Frankie,' replied Bony, and gave the details.

'Looking for a horse? That old scroundrel wouldn't go looking for a horse. He'd send his bucks. Wanted to look you over, that's what. Where were you when he sort of called to pass the time of day?'

Bony told him as nearly as he could, and they went on southward, Bony's camels nose-lined to Newton's rear beast. Bony walked on the far side of the Fence with the pitchfork to toss over isolated buckbush. The two men camped at sundown at the turn off to the grass shed.

On settling down for the evening smoke beside the

bright camp fire, Bony decided to take Newton further into his confidence. He told him what he had discovered at Bore Nine and his deductions from it.

'Putting yourself in the overseer's place, wouldn't you have expected those blacks to report their ideas about that fire?' asked Bony.

'Yes, I certainly would. They would know that the overseer evidently didn't draw the picture right. It's funny, Ed, Posthole Frankie ain't slow in coming forward. Neither of 'em could have said anything to the police because the sergeant and his offsider never went there to work it out. They took it for granted that Maidstone continued straight for Bore Ten, and took the overseer's word for it that Maidstone merely boiled water for tea at Bore Nine and took a picture or two.'

'Do King Moses or his Medicine Man get about much? Does the tribe walkabout much or little on this Fence?'

'Not as much as they did before the Monster frightened 'em off. They get about a good deal, though, at certain times.' Newton used a fire-stick a yard long to light his pipe. 'The last time I seen them out this way would be about three months back.'

'Have many of them possessed rifles?' pressed Bony.

'Hard to tell. Several I know. When they was out this way last time one fired at an eagle, missed and nearly hit Nugget on a sandhill. Nugget went crook about it to me, and I complained to Moses when next I saw him. Fact is that the young bucks work a bit for

the station and spend their money on a rifle traded by
the Syrian hawker. Should be stopped. You can buy
a rifle as easily as a tin of milk, even if you've never
fired one in your life.'

'Nugget must have been fairly close to that bullet
for him to report it to you,' Bony said. 'He could have
been murdered. Maidstone could equally well have
been killed by accident, by an abo firing indiscrimin-
ately. Were that so, then their dumbness is easily explained. They don't act without good reason. There is
always a good reason for placing the ban of silence on
a lubra. They are ever logical, we must concede.'

'Yes, it could have been an accident. I can't see 'em
shooting Maidstone just for the sport of it.''

This was a new angle which fitted nicely into the
problem of non-co-operation by the aborigines, and it
was worth considering and investigating. Absence of
motive was certainly puzzling.

'When an abo is ordered to be dumb he can be a
fair bastard,' continued Newton. 'Them abos was
ordered to be dumb. Not only the two with Joyce, but
them over at Lake Frome. Now who was it put the
ban of silence on the flaming lot? Charlie the Nut,
of course! He was with Joyce when they found the
body.'

'The Medicine Man would then have only to wink
an eyelid and all the Lake Frome abos would be in-
capable of speech,' Bony supplemented. 'He wouldn't
do that to protect a white man, which strengthens the
supposition that an aborigine shot Maidstone, in which

case it is hard to imagine that it was anything other than an accident, for robbery was certainly not the motive. Nothing of value was taken from Maidstone's possession.'

'Might have been, but it's pretty hard to see just how an accident like that could happen, unless some shortsighted abo thought he was a kangaroo.'

'But accident or not, I've got to unearth the killer. Since that day all the aborigines on both sides of the Fence have been sitting down and doing nothing. They wouldn't even talk about it among themselves. The subject is taboo, and no amount of examination, even on Gestapo lines, would make them talk.

'I have been presented with similar situations, and not only by aborigine conspiracy,' Bony went on. 'When a calculating murderer merely sits and does nothing, he takes a heck of a lot of budging. It is the same when a number of people are concerned. They're like rabbits in a burrow, and the only method to use in order to shift them is to stir them up into taking action, taking action through fear of the daylight. I want you to do something for me.'

'Name it, Ed.'

'When we get to Quinambie, I want you to drop a sly hint or two that you suspect I'm a detective at work on the Maidstone case, making sure that the blacks hear of it. At the same time do a little boasting for me that shortly I will make an arrest. You work out your approach between now and then.'

'Just give hints?'

'That's it. The line being that I'm doing little else but talk about the killing and constantly questioning you about this aborigine and that, including Nugget. Make up a sly yarn.'

Newton burst into low laughter, and as abruptly became silent. He was thoughtful for several minutes before pointing out the obvious.

'Mightn't it be a bit dangerous for you?' he said. 'Living like we do they could put a full stop after you. There's no one here to guard your rear, and another accident could easily happen without stirring up much suspicion.'

'It's a chance I have to take. I shall not like it, you may depend, but I've a job to do beside forking buckbush over your Fence.'

'All right, I'll start off the rumours, but personally I wouldn't like having to look over my shoulder a thousand times a day. And what about the nights?'

'Don't worry about it. Before murder is deliberately done there is a long approach, and it is during the long approach that the threatened person may take counteraction.'

Bony rose to put water into a billy for bedtime tea. The occasional clang of a camel bell told the story that they had finished feeding and were also settling down for the night. A meteor flamed across the sky and a mopoke rendered its funereal cry. After that the night was completely silent, so that when the men arranged their blankets on the ground sheets it was a rustle in the vast stillness.

Commander Joyce was still without a book-keeper, and it was he who served them with the foodstuffs they required from the store. He was told of the plan Bony had arranged with Newton and he liked it no more than Newton had. Later on, when Bony visited the station cook with his meat-bag, Newton dallied in pretence of fixing his gear.

'Good day-ee, Ed!' greeted the cook. 'How's the guts?'

'Recovered by next day. How are things with you?'

'Okay, Ed. Still toiling hard. How did you like the windstorm the other day? When she blows, she blows, eh?' The cook whisked away the cheesecloth covering the side of beef and slashed into it with his butcher's knife – expertly, too. With about twenty pounds of beef, Bony went back to the camelmen's camp behind the machinery shed and a moment or so later Newton proceeded to collect his ration of meat. Bony saw Post-hole Frankie leave the horse yards and almost follow Newton into the kitchen, and when the overseer did not soon appear, he smiled a little grimly and could imagine Newton 'putting over' the sly hints.

Nothing was said on the way out to the cane-grass shed where the camels were freed, and the salting of the major portion of the meat undertaken.

'Frankie didn't miss a word,' Newton then said. 'Looked everywhere but at me and the cook. He got it all right. I told 'em about you when the cook wanted to know how you were shaping on the Fence. Said you was a newchum Fence worker. Said you were as full of questions as a butcher's dog's full of meat. Cook says you're too educated to be a real bush worker, and that gave me another chance to tell 'em it was my opinion and that I'm inclined to bet you're a policeman in disguise. The cook said he knew the police wouldn't give up the Maidstone killing all that easy, and that he wouldn't take my bet if I made one. All that good-oh with you?'

'Excellent,' Bony replied. 'Posthole Frankie will go that fast to Moses and his Medicine Man that no one will see him for dust.'

'The cook made it easy for me. I didn't say about you lookin' to make an arrest. Didn't think it was necessary. Think them abos will begin moving?'

'No, not for some time. The elders will have a council meeting over Moses's little fire, and then Charlie the Nut will go into his act and communicate with his opposite number at Lake Frome. You probably won't believe it, but it will be done by smoke signal and telepathy. I shall find the future interesting.'

Newton chuckled, saying: 'Good word, interesting! I know another good word, alarming!'

'Why call that feller Charlie the Nut?'

'Don't know. Never thought to ask. White-man's nickname for someone they don't understand, probably. I know why Frankie is called Posthole. Because that was his job for a month. Went crook at it, too. Rather ride a horse, like all of 'em, but Joyce told him he could gouge postholes or get off the station; seems no one argues with Joyce.'

85

They parted the next morning, Newton going south and expecting to meet with Nugget and Company to whom he would say nothing of his suspicions that Ed Bonnay was a detective. Bony returned to routine work on the Fence, but was never far from his rifle.

Two days passed before Moses made his first move. It was a windless morning and Bony, who was working on high ground, saw the smoke signal far beyond Bore Nine. The natives at Lake Frome homestead would see only the top portion of the disjointed smoke column, which would be enough for their Chief or Medicine Man to go into a huddle. Then there would be much talk about two little fires.

Bony fired the first shot, but not at a human being. He was crossing the series of gigantic sand ranges and coming to the summit of one when he saw on the flat beyond a dingo being attacked by two eagles. The dingo was getting the worst of it. A bird flying low along the flat would knock the dog off its feet, and before the animal could stand to run the other eagle swept in to knock it down with a wing pinion. So it went on, each bird taking its turn, sweeping in upon the victim, buffeting with each charge, and never once striking the ground with a claw.

Somewhere in the vicinity would be the eagles' nest. Built high in the topmost fork of a dead tree, it would permit a landscape view to eyes which could see a bush rat from a couple of miles high. The dog ought not to have been caught in the open in daylight, and should it get out of this situation it would never be caught again. Bony knew, however, that it would never escape these two birds, who would continue their attack until the dog lay dying of sheer exhaustion. Taking aim, Bony mercifully shot it and the birds departed in large, unhurried, upward circles.

The report of the point-44-calibre rifle reverberated along the corridors of the ranges and Bony wondered at what distance it would be heard by man.

Being low in water and his camels edgy from thirst, he left making camp until his return from the bore lake. With the rifle slung across a shoulder, his train passed into South Australia and it had proceeded but half the distance to the bore lake when Old George's bell warned him the animal had broken away. George seemed determined to get to the lake ahead of Bony, and his bell clanked rapidly as he drew ahead. Bony made no attempt to catch him, for in so doing he would have had to leave Rosie free.

When he reached the lake George was standing with hind legs wide apart and still drinking. He ranged Rosie alongside George and when both had taken their fill, he hooshed them down to chew cud. Then he had to unload George to get at the well-nigh empty drums, and after that he got out a roll of line to make a new nose-line for George. He had cut the length of light rope and was affixing to one end the loop of twine to slip about the nose-plug when both animals abruptly stood. Both turned about and away from the lake and Bony had time to notice that Old George stood between him and the rifle leaning against a water-drum.

Coming at high speed was the largest camel Bony had ever seen. The sudden chill that went through Bony only strengthened his sudden realization that this was the Lake Frome Monster !

*Chapter Nine*

# The Monster

The beast ploughed across the sandy desert like a ship in a rough sea. It seemed to have but two legs, when actually it had four. The nearside legs lifted off the ground at the same instant and then down they came and the offside legs lifted clear. The body was dark brown at the summit, light brown near the legs. The head was kept low and the impression was one of extreme viciousness.

Bony attempted to rush around Old George, but George moved, and as he did so prevented him from reaching the rifle. On turning again, the Monster was upon him.

With astonishing alacrity, the beast skidded to a halt to blow its breath into Bony's face. From it came a long, gurgling, high-pitched moan which seemed to enclose him and his two camels within a barrier beyond which all the world was sunk into slumberous peace. Actuated rather by the instinct of a camelman than by logical thought, Bony flicked the new nose-line over the beast's snout, caught the opposite end and pulled downward.

'Hoosta! Hoosta!' he shouted, and tugged violently on the line. The Monster drew in its uvula, which had been protruding, and the glare of hate vanished from its eyes. It sank to its knees, went down on its back legs, which it tucked against its belly. Its head jerked up, and up the long neck rose the cud which it masticated almost violently.

Bony heard grunts behind him and knew that his two camels had also obeyed the order to lie down. He felt a reaction which made him tremble, but knew also that fear had fled into the distant mirage.

'Now wasn't that something?' he asked the Lake Frome Monster. 'I'm a lucky man, and so are you because had I been able to get to the rifle you would have been laid out for good. Damn it, I believe all you wanted was society, gentle companionship. You've been ill-treated, cast out, shot at, turned into a national Ishmael. Well, we'll see. You've lost your nose-plug so I'll make you a bridle until I can rope you to a tree to put in another, and you take it for granted that if you play up, go on strike or misbehave, I'll shoot you for certain sure.'

The Monster continued cud-chewing. He did not move his head when Bony's deft hands wove the bridle with a length of nose-line rope, and when Bony leaned against his hump his hide didn't twitch.

Bony lit a cigarette and surveyed the situation. He didn't need a third camel, and the two he had were good campers until lack of water to moisten cud drove them to seek it. However, this newcomer, unlikely to be owned by anyone, was a strong bullock in its prime, whereas Old George was really too old to carry the load demanded of him. Overseer Newton would probably object to taking another camel on the strength, particularly one with the reputation as a killer that the Monster had rightly or wrongly acquired. However, he might not if the Monster was broken to take a pack saddle. There were many other ifs, but Bony decided to give the Monster a chance.

It was not possible to anticipate how the Monster would behave when the man left him, but Bony had to do that to claim his rifle and load the water-drums on to Old George. He stepped away from the hump, reached the rifle, and the Monster merely continued to chew cud with great content. The drums loaded, Old George was given a new nose-line and ordered to his feet. Rosie got up when he did and the end of George's nose-line was fastened to the rear of the riding saddle. The Monster got up without haste, still chewing, and the length of nose-line dangling from his bridle was hitched to George's load. He behaved perfectly all the way to the spot where Bony intended camping for the night.

He put the camels down where he had camped with Needle Kent, unloaded, stood the animals up and hobbled them. He had straps and hobble chains as spares, and with the set he approached the Monster to hobble short his forelegs.

Here was the most dangerous job to do with an unknown animal. It meant stooping low to the ground right at the animal's large padded feet armed with large toenails. The man would then be at the mercy of the camel, who might strike or bite with crippling effect, and in circumstances which could well prove fatal when in such complete isolation.

The Monster was standing. It was no use hesitating. Bony placed his hand on the animal's shoulder, then lowered the hand down the foreleg, stooping while doing this until the beast was towering over him. He had to reach behind the nearer leg to put a strap about the farther leg, finally putting the other strap about the nearer. The Monster never moved.

'Well, I must say, you're a perfect ruddy gentleman,' he observed standing away. 'Anyone would think you have been working under a load all day instead of rampaging up and down the eastern half of South Australia for months, perhaps years. But don't ever forget that should you play up, I'll lay you out cold.'

The Monster was with his two camels when he went for them, and he followed George back to camp where Bony laid him down against a stout tree for the final indignity. With a pack rope he drew the Monster's head hard against the tree, and with agile fingers slipped a new nose-plug up inside the nostril and the small end out through the hole punctured to take it. The Monster objected only to the extent of barely showing its uvula, and was then released from the tree.

Now with harness in order and taking the last place on the train, the Monster gave no trouble. As Bony worked on the summits of the sand ranges, he kept an eye on the Monster all that day. Thereafter, he did not worry about him. The Monster appeared to have no designs on his life.

It was early in the afternoon while Bony was working on the South Australian side of the Fence that he saw three horsemen approaching, and a minute later he could distinguish that one was white. He introduced himself as Levvey, the manager of Lake Frome Station.

The two aborigines with him had fallen to his rear as he rode up to Bony. His eyes were small but unblinking in their concentration and, as always, a slight smile widened his thick lips.

'Day, Ed. You see any cattle out this way?'

'Not for some time,' Bony replied, and reached for his tobacco tin and papers. Levvey dismounted and followed suit.

'Any at the bore when you were there?'

'Didn't see any. I was there four days ago.'

'Might be farther south. Want to turn 'em west.' Blue eyes shrewdly looked over the fenceman. 'How's the job going?'

'Not too bad. Plenty to keep me occupied.'

Levvey looked through the wire at the three camels lying down at ease but offered no remark about the third one. He lounged with his back to a fence post, and in appearance was no different from Newton or from Bony. He smiled readily, and seemed to take life easily.

'Still not much of a job barbering this Fence,' he said casually, and Bony waited for what was coming.

'Slogging your guts out after every windstorm. The loneliness would drive me screwy. You want a change of job see me. Done much cattle work?'

'Fair bit in my time. As you say the job's tough after a storm, but the pay is good, and I don't intend to stay on it long.'

'Think it over, Ed. I got to work with abos, and they get tired too often. I could use a man of your stamp, but don't tell Newton I said so. What with the Frome Monster, if there is one, which I doubt, and schoolteachers getting themselves murdered, the abos are afraid to move about unless kicked in the backside.'

'Could have been an accident – the schoolteacher, I mean.'

'An accident! Never thought of it like that.' Levvey dropped the butt of his cigarette and rolled another. 'How d'you make that out?'

'Well, didn't an abo nearly shoot Nugget? Newton told me he almost got it.'

'Yes, so he did. We was talking about it and reckon they can get guns too easy. Come to think of it, they can. I told one of my abos that if he didn't take care, I'll take it off him. Careless bastard. Maidstone could have been shot accidentally. Don't seem no reason to shoot him. Didn't rob him or anything.'

Levvey did not appear to be in any hurry to go on. Bony said:

'I was in the Hill when it happened. Papers full of it. Police didn't think it was an accident, but what else could it have been?'

'What else, as you say, Ed. People don't get murdered without a reason, and there was no reason for that murder. You ever done any police work?'

'Done a bit of tracking for them a couple of times. Could have joined them, but I get itchy feet. The abos didn't do any good on the murder case, did they?'

'No, they didn't pick up any tracks of a man about the bore exceptin' them left by Maidstone. By gee! It could have been an accident. Of course, to be fair the abos didn't have much time before the wind came and wiped even the cattle tracks out.'

'Interesting subject.'

'Too right,' agreed Levvey. 'Well, I'd better get on. When d'you reckon you'll be seeing Newton again?'

'Can't rightly say.'

'Of course not, Ed. Anyway, you want a job let me know. Wife's a good cook. Give you good quarters.' Levvey mounted, nodded, gave a see-you-later, and departed with his two henchmen. Bony had finished work here, and he climbed the Fence, roused his somnolent camels and also departed to the south.

He wondered about Jack Levvey, who conformed to a bush type. Levvey had come up the hard way and would know his work as well as managing a gang of aborigines. He would be able to track as well as they, but whether he had done any tracking at the scene of the murder was not on record. Probably not, as he would avoid losing face with Commander Joyce.

Levvey had accepted the accident theory as fitting the facts known to him, and Bony was beginning to regard this theory with some seriousness. The failure of the aborigines to locate the tracks of a man between the Fence and the bore lake might mean that in truth there were none to see. The shot might have been fired east of the Ten-Mile gate, either by an aborigine or by either Nugget or Needle Kent. Either of the latter could have fired the shot through the netting, and then, to avoid leaving tracks anywhere about the lake or the dead man, have gone for water to Bore Nine, several miles deep into New South Wales.

Nugget could not be excluded from responsibility although known to possess a Savage rifle. It was still not proven that he did not have a Winchester in his gear. The accident theory would have to be tested.

Working his way southward, eventually Bony came to the turn-off to Quinambie homestead, passed it and when camped at the bottom end of his section met Nugget and his tribe coming northward and headed to the cane-grass shed.

'How you going, Ed?' was Nugget's greeting.

'Pretty well. Bit of work to do after the windstorm, but Mount Everest escaped damage.'

Nugget and those with him were greatly interested in the Monster.

'He joined the party at Bore Ten and refused to leave us, and so I brought him along,' replied Bony. 'Quiet enough. Reckon he'd do better work than Old George who is a bit of a worry without water.'

'What I told the boss,' asserted Nugget, at the moment engaged slicing a tobacco plug for his pipe.

'Should of pensioned Old George off years ago. Levvey said he's seen you. Had a natter, he said.'

The dark eyes were directed to Bony, and Nugget waited for possible enlightenment as to what had been said.

Bony carelessly told him that Levvey was after cattle to push westward and left it at that. The lubras went on with the camels, following Bony's section to the turn-off. One would be about forty, the other in her twenties. The children went with them. Bony had noticed a rifle in a canvas gun-case slung from the riding camel's saddle, and shrewdly guessed it was the Savage so dear to the heart of its owner.

He also noticed that at the approach of Nugget's party the Monster evidenced growing restlessness. At first he thought this was due to the coming of strange camels, and then that it was caused by the women. Bony had known of a camel who behaved badly at the sight of a woman's skirt, and of yet another who would bolt at the sight of a man on horseback. Nugget was saying:

'Jack Levvey told me you reckon the murder could of been an accident. Said you might be right.'

'Weren't you nearly shot one time?' queried Bony.

'Too right, Ed. Bullet went past me that close I heard it. Come across the feller that fired it, and felt like giving him a hiding.' Nugget laughed, and Bony failed to see the reason. 'Bloody blackfellers shouldn't be allowed a rifle. I told Newton about it and he agreed.'

*Chapter Ten*

# Testing Needle Kent

Once again at the northern end of his section, Bony proceeded to test the theory of accident. Standing at the Bore Ten gate he found the ground clear enough to see through the trees to the stakes marking the place where Maidstone had fallen. He could not see the bore or its lake of water, as the trees to his left were too close together where they merged against the slope of the sand range. By walking northwards from the gate, at a hundred yards distance he obtained a still clearer view of the stakes and from there he could see the lake as well.

Assuming that Maidstone was walking back to his camp, a shooter at this hundred yards' point could hardly fail to see him unless absorbed by the sight of a bunch of kangaroos, but if at the gate among the closer-growing trees the shooter was aiming at a 'roo, it was possible not to notice the man beyond them. All the shooter had to do was to slip the rifle barrel through the netting, take careful aim and fire. That he missed the kangaroos and hit the man could have been due to haste when the kangaroos were on the run. Summing up, Bony decided that an accident was possible, if not probable.

It was late on the day before Needle Kent was to meet the Lake Frome utility with his ration list that Needle arrived to shout his greeting before it was necessary and, having gulped the pannikin of tea waiting for him, he and Bony combined forces and proceeded to the lake. Needle was curious about the extra camel and was given the explanation passed on to Nugget. The sun was setting when, having watered the animals and filled the drums and taken a bathe, they returned to the camp and settled at the camp fire.

It was remarkable the amount of gossip they had to exchange, what with Bony's meetings first with Levvey and then with Nugget, and with Needle's story of his work and of the iguana that stole the remains of a cold stew he had forgotten to cover. When the stars were out and the bells were telling of the direction in which the camels were feeding, Bony opened with his questioning:

'Did you fire through the netting at a kangaroo hereabouts?'

'Don't remember. Why?'

'At that time Maidstone was shot?'

'Don't think so. No, I didn't. What's on your mind?'

'Nothing much. What do you do at night before turning in?'

'Talks to meself, I think. You know, bakes a damper for the next day, makes a stew for breakfast, all that.'

'It's the same with me, but I haven't yet arrived at

talking to myself. I will do if I stay on the Fence for long. I've been looking around and thinking about the Maidstone murder, and I'm thinking now it was an accident. I'm trying to prove it was, for something to do.'

Needle took time to absorb this problem of something to occupy the mind after the day's work. Bony rolled a cigarette, lit it with an ember at the point of a fire-stick before saying :

'Well, if you stand at the gate you can see the stakes marking where Maidstone was walking back to camp. Let's say that beyond the gate was a nice fat kangaroo. The feller with the rifle wanted meat and he's so excited about getting the 'roo that he fires without seeing Maidstone, misses the 'roo and hits the man.'

'It could of been that way,' Needle agreed, interest making his normally high-pitched voice rise even higher. 'The police didn't argue that out as far's I know. That's the way it must have been, Ed. No one's thought it out like that. There's no motive for it. Maidstone being the stranger he didn't have no enemies up around here. Yes, Ed, you could be right at that.'

'I think the police took too much for granted,' softly commented Bony. 'They mixed the dates for one thing, and for another they didn't have the trackers working this side of the Fence. Supposing a party of Quinambie abos were out this way. Some of them have rifles. Supposing one of them fired through the fence at something, missed whatever it was and accidentally killed

Maidstone. Wouldn't that account for them missing out on the tracking before the wind came? Supposing you were the abo with the rifle, what would you have done?'

'Gone for me flamin' life!' was Needle's prompt reply.

'Wouldn't you have gone to see if the man you hit was actually dead?'

'I'd have watched from the Fence to see if he moved before doing a get. But you made out I was an abo, and I'm telling you what an abo would do. Anyway, about them abos falling down on the tracking job, remember the cattle came down the Fence and blotted out the tracks. They blotted out my tracks when I went with my camels for water.'

'You think the cattle would have watered at the place where we watered?'

'They'd break away from the Fence about here and make for the lake, same as we do. It would be dark, and the duffers wouldn't see Maidstone's camp, or Maidstone alive or dead.'

'We seem to be out of joint,' Bony said cautiously. 'I think you are wrong on your dates.'

'How so?'

'Let's work it out this way, Needle. Maidstone left Quinambie homestead after lunch on June Eighth. Joyce understood he'd make for the Lake Frome homestead, but Maidstone camped for that night at Bore Nine. Next day he went on to Bore Ten and camped there that night. Very early the next day the cattle passed you at some place up the Fence, and so, as you say, the cattle would veer off the Fence at about here, and the duffers would see Maidstone's camp.

'So that very early on the morning of June Tenth Maidstone was in camp near Bore Ten with a cold fire, and the duffers were heading their cattle towards the bore lake. Then there is the man with the rifle. If the accident theory is correct, he was at the gate when Maidstone was coming back from the lake with his billy early on the same morning, but before the cattle were veered from the Fence to blot out his tracks and your own.'

'That would be about it, Ed,' Needle said, trapped into an admission that he was lying when he had insisted that he was camped at the Ten-Mile along his section when the duffers passed. He even confirmed the admission. 'Yes, I was at the Five-Mile that night. I wonder if the abo with the rifle was there to meet them duffers?'

'It's possible, Needle. But hardly likely. Having accidentally shot Maidstone, he wouldn't hang about but go off back to Quinambie and report to Moses or Charlie the Nut. So we arrive back at the point that it was an accident.'

Needle Kent beamed agreement, produced a pipe and filled it with cigarette tobacco.

'You got a education,' he said. 'All that works her out good.'

'Too good, Needle. I wouldn't like you to tell it to Newton, or to Levvey, or to anyone. Let the police

102

work it out. That's what they are paid for. And we
don't want to be associated with those cattle and the
duffers, do we?'

'Not on your life, Ed.'

'Only Newton knows what you told him and he
promised to keep it to himself. Or rather he promised
to keep you out of it.'

Needle now gave proof that he wasn't 100 per cent
*non compos mentis* when he asked how Bony knew
that Maidstone had indeed camped at Bore Nine.
Bony told him he'd gone for water and found the
remains of a large camp fire, and of the empty matchbox which was not purchased at the Quinambie store.

'Without the matchbox it could be said that that
night fire had been lit by Nugget or one of his family,'
he explained. 'Anyway, you keep that under your hat.
It isn't important.'

'Trust me, Ed. Yes, you worked her out fine. You
should have been a "d". Cousin of mine was a policeman down in Melbourne. Got up to detective-sergeant.
Had a gift for it.'

Bony studied Needle as he rattled on about his
policeman cousin and thoughtfully reappraised this
human skeleton. He felt he had at last straightened
out the background which had never been clear and
altered constantly. Needle had claimed to have been
at various mileages on the night of June Ninth, most
likely to confuse the story of the passing cattle, in his
determination to have nothing to do with rustlers.

The record was now clear, and facts were related

logically to facts. Maidstone had arrived at Bore Ten on June Ninth and had decided to take pictures that night at the bore lake. That night also Needle Kent was camped five miles north of the gate, not two miles or ten miles. Again on that night rustlers drove cattle past Needle's cold fire at two in the morning. They had at this time to drive the cattle five miles to the gate plus one mile to the lake. South of the gate by six miles were Nugget and his family – if Nugget could be believed.

If Nugget could be believed! Having established to his own satisfaction where Needle was on that vital night, Bony would have to examine whether Nugget could be believed or not.

Here indeed was a crime seemingly without a motive. It was tempting to accept the theory of accidental shooting. Many a man, Bony knew, had been mistaken for a wallaby or kangaroo in bush or when the light was bad, and shot as such, even in shooting parties when one would expect to come on human beings. Out here, one would not ordinarily expect anything that moved to be human. The mystery was made difficult of solution by the very paucity of suspects. A perfect stranger comes among these few suspects and for no apparent reason is killed. That the rustlers had anything to do with it was very unlikely, because they would be the last to draw attention to their activities, which require the stealth and swift action associated with robbing a bank vault at night.

Those rustlers knew they had a clear run to Bore

Ten and beyond at a point where the stolen cattle would be out of sight of the fencemen. Levvey had told Needle that he would not be going to Quinambie as he had work to do westward of his homestead. He and his riders would be far distant from travelling stock coming down the Fence far to the eastward. In fact, the two operations would be separated by some ninety miles. Someone must have informed the rustlers that on one or two nights they would have a clear run. Needle, for one, knew it, and doubtless Joyce's overseer would know it, as well as Charlie the Nut and his chief, and Nugget and his people.

Needle concluded his story about his cousin and got up to pour water into a billy for tea. This action broke off Bony's reflections. He allowed sufficient time to elapse to create the impression that he had been listening intently to Needle and then said :

'You don't keep a diary, Needle, and so how do you keep track of the days to get you down here in time to meet Levvey with the ration list?'

'Easy, Ed. I read in a book once that a bloke kept time by notching a stick. Every night before turning in I notches a stick, starting from the day I leave here. I forgot twice and had to go into Quinambie for the rations and meat.'

'You would follow the track passing Bore Nine? How far off that track is Bore Six?'

'Seven miles when you're about four from the homestead.'

'Have you been to Bore Six?' pressed Bony.

105

'Never no cause to. The blacks camp there most times.'

'D'you know how long Nugget has had his Savage?'

'Got her off the hawker last time he was at Quinambie. Lemme think. That would be just a month before the murder. Like me, he had a Winchester forty-four before that.'

At that stage the water for the tea boiled, and soon the two men were rolled in their blankets. It was the next morning that Bony continued to press the subject of Nugget's rifle.

'Did Nugget do anything with the Winchester?'

'Couldn't say, Ed. Sold it to the blacks most likely. They're always tradin' something. Funny thing about the abos. One buys a pair of pants and next week another's wearin' 'em. Same with rifles. One gets a rifle and every Tom, Dick and bloody Harry of 'em is shootin' with it.'

'And one of them nearly shot Nugget?'

'He come close to it, Ed. Nugget went dead crook.'

'When was that?'

'Oh, some time before Nugget bought his Savage.'

'Then don't you think that Nugget would be reluctant to sell a Winchester to the blacks? It was, I think, Newton who said Nugget said the abos shouldn't be allowed to have rifles.'

'Then probably Nugget's still got his Winchester. Mind you, I'm not sure about it. I'll make the tea. He could have given it to Mary. You know, or perhaps you don't, Mary's his wife's sister. Good-looking young

lubra about twenty-five. She'd have to run like hell if
I caught her in the open.'

'She might shoot you.'

'She might at that. Got the name for being a good
shot.' Needle pondered for a moment, then chuckled
before adding: 'Still I'd chance it. Sounds like Jack
Levvey's coming.'

The Lake Frome utility came through the gateway
to stop within yards of the camp, and Needle handed
over his list. Levvey waved to Bony. Three male
aborigines in the back were silent among themselves,
but they watched only Bony as the vehicle drew away
on the track to Quinambie.

*Chapter Eleven*

# The Playful Aborigines

It was mid-afternoon when the day darkened. For several days there had not been a cloud in the sky, and now Bony looked up expecting to see the sun wearing a mask. The sun shone brilliantly as usual, but the daylight had waned. It was not due to a change of country, as sometimes happens when one passes from open bluebush to dead herbal rubbish amid box trees growing on grey flats.

Bony was walking beside his Fence, the nose-line of the leading camel slung from an arm, the bell of the rear animal tolling its rhythmical tune. The day was normal, the surroundings now familiar and nothing seemed out of place. There was a post needing replacement, and Bony put his camels down, felled a mulga, removed the rotted post from the wires, erected the new post and wired it into position. The operation cost thirty minutes of time.

This job done, Bony leaned against the hump of the Frome Monster, and fashioned a cigarette. The day continued brightly but it had not recovered its normal stereoscopic brilliance. Shadows were as sharply outlined as usual, and yet there seemed to be a pervading shadow over everything in this normal world.

Thoughtfully and unhurriedly, Bony smoked his cigarette, and having done so he stubbed out the remaining ash and pocketed the butt. The effect of the change of light was certainly in himself. It was not dissimilar to an abrupt attack of mental depression. It could be due to a threatening stomach disorder, but there was as yet no feeling of such a physical upset as might be occasioned by the bore water. He had to recognize the possibility of mental disturbance.

Once again on patrol, automatically noting the passage of the endless Fence, Bony pondered on the probability that the aborigines had begun their opening move. Somewhere amid these vast spaces in which one human being would occupy ten square miles or more, a man, or two men, perhaps three, would be squatting over a very small fire. They would be old men long past the age when they would be expected to be physically active in the conduct of the tribe, men having been inducted into secrets handed down for a thousand generations and skilful in practices which only fear of the white man's law and way of life had but recently blunted.

When Bony first came to Quinambie and the Border Fence, the aborigines had been sittim-down-do-nothing. Then he had deliberately prodded them into action by having Newton publish the suspicion that he was a policeman in disguise. And now having occupied several days and nights with discussion, it had been decided to be rid of him. They had a secret which he might uncover.

How would the men crouching over their little fire argue about him? What was their point of view? Like the whites he was an itinerant bush worker; that is, on the surface. He was thought to be a policeman but there was no proof of it, and thus persuasion not violence would be adopted. To begin with, anyway.

So they crouched over their little fire and united the power of their wills to disturb the balance of his mind. The purpose was to subjugate him to intimidation precisely as the hypnotist prepares his subject to accept his commands.

Provided the bore water did not eventually have unpleasant results, then Bony felt sure he was becoming the subject of thought transference and would be the victim of extremely subtle assault. Proof would be provided that the aborigines did have something to hide, and that something must be the manner of the death of Maidstone. It was possible, but only faintly possible, that Nugget resented being transferred from one section to another and had persuaded his tribe so to act. The point to be admitted without equivocation was that he, Bony, was half aborigine and that his aboriginal half was much stronger than the white ancestry in his make-up. Thus he was as open to victimization as a full blood.

Bony knew that it was fear that killed: fear killed many of his people in spite of all that medical science could do to save them. He also knew that doctors everywhere were finding more and more connections between physical symptoms and mental and emotional upsets. He also knew well that thought could be transmitted – instances of telepathy over vast distances were a well-established fact. But he also knew that he was still of his race and countless centuries of acceptance of the fact that a man must die when the bone was pointed at him was still strong in him. It was more than the case of the intellectual who still refused to walk under the ladder because his parents had told him it was unlucky. He had felt this conflict between his intellect and his emotions before. Once before he had suffered the five bones and the eagle's claws of the boning apparatus being pointed at him. This was when he had fallen foul of the Kalchut tribe while trying to find the killer of a man who had foully misused members of that tribe. This time he was not prepared to submit to the sprinkling of the powder which the natives used symbolically to open up the bodies of their victims so that the magic transmitted by the bones might the more easily enter. This time he was not prepared to undergo the conflict within himself that followed and the hovering between life and death which only outside intervention had ended in his favour. Certainly he would probably not voluntarily give up the will to live, but even the depression and lassitude which would inevitably follow the first stages of the boning would be enough to hinder his judgement when he needed it to be at its most acute.

One thing was on his side. He knew that in these

days when the aborigines knew that the death of any individual, black or white, brought probings and questions and possibly charges of murder, the decision to point the bone would only be taken after due deliberation round the camp fire, and not until round that very fire one of the *mauia* stones in which the potent magic employed in bone-pointing resided had been carefully ground and sufficient particles produced to enable the dust to be sprinkled over a sleeping Bonaparte.

'There is only one way,' he thought to himself. 'I must stop this at the source. If the kind of life I have lived has taught me anything,' he pondered, 'one thing has been self-evident, one must always face one's fear and never suppress it.'

He sat in solemn thought for a moment. Suddenly he remembered something he had forgotten to do on the day he had left his home. He went over to his battered suitcase and fumbled in the pocket of the sports coat which he had discarded when he had donned the working clothes he wore on the Fence.

It took only a few minutes to saddle Rosie and after making a few preparations, Bony was on his way to Quinambie. It was a long and tiring ride, and the more difficult because he didn't know exactly where the aborigines were camped and he certainly didn't want to call at the homestead and so give the alarm. It was important that it should be dark when he arrived and to find the camp site would be difficult, even had he known exactly where it was. Even then he might not be able to find Old Moses and the Medicine Man, whom he felt sure were at the bottom of the attempt to injure him which was now being planned.

Bonaparte made a wide circle round Quinambie until he picked up a trail which indicated that workmen had travelled to and from the station. He followed a course parallel to the trail until he came to a collection of bark and galvanized shanties. This, he thought, must be where the tribe lived. There was almost a full moon and the camp showed little sign of life apart from dogs slinking round the huts. Bony stopped and looked round him until he saw a convenient clump of mulga trees and there he dismounted and tethered Rosie. He had noted that there was a series of high rocky outcrops behind the camp and here, he thought, if anywhere, would be the retreat of the Medicine Man and his helpers. Cautiously he worked his way towards these outcrops. Suddenly, as he crossed the first outcrop he saw that a gully ran in front of him and turned slightly behind the ridge.

Bony crept as silently as he knew, using the moonlight as far as possible to avoid treading on sticks, or dried bark which would crackle. Although it was a cold night he felt perspiration on the palms of his hands and knew that the fear which was his heritage was walking with him. Suddenly, he stopped sharply. The smoke of a small fire was rising from behind a huge rock. Silently he worked his way until he could see without being seen. There, round a small fire, were three aborigines, completely naked except for a fringe of feathers attached to their feet. As their bodies glistened in the

113

firelight, so they gazed intently into the small fire, while one, whom he took to be Charlie, the Medicine Man, slowly scraped particles from a small stone on to a piece of bark lying in front of him. Not a muscle moved in any of the three faces, which could have been carved of stone. The power of their concentration was so intense that Bony also felt his breath loud in his throat and breathing was almost difficult. All at once he felt foolish and inadequate. Here he was, face-to-face with an age-old ceremony, which neither he nor the white men for whom he worked and among whom he lived would ever understand. His plans seemed trivial and childish, but somehow he knew he must break the power of that concentration – somehow, no matter the consequences, he must make this ceremony seem ridiculous. His limbs felt as if they had leaden weights attached and it was only with a supreme effort of will that he forced himself on. Noiselessly, he approached until he was hidden behind the nearest rock not five yards from the fire. There was no change in the trance-like state of the three seated round the fire. Suddenly, Bony put a hand in his pocket and threw a paper packet over the heads of the fire-sitters. The packet fell into the fire with a soft 'wuff'. The three startled natives jumped to their feet, and then a firecracker started to explode, scattering the fire in all directions. Still with the fear of the spirits of darkness that they were invoking in their hearts, the three natives fled.

Bony felt the tension go out of his body. The packet

he had promised to his youngest son and forgotten to give him before he had left home had scattered the forces of evil with the embers of the fire. Once broken by ridicule, Bony felt that no more attempts would be made to kill him by pointing the bone at him. Indifferent now as to what eyes were watching him, he returned to Rosie and rode back to his camp.

## Chapter Twelve

# The Attack is Switched

On his way back to camp Bony shot a kangaroo to provide himself with fresh meat for the following day. After a full day's work on the Fence he camped at sundown and made the usual cooking fire. He washed in two pints of water and after giving the suddy liquid to Old George, dined off salt beef and damper, with jam on the damper for the sweet. The camels wandered off for their dinner and aided by the firelight he baked a damper for the next day. The stars shone without winking, a cool wind came from the south, and nothing happened to disturb the peace of night. Bony sighed and relaxed. His depression had lifted. No longer was his tribal ancestry being used against him.

Old George was a good camper. At the end of a day carrying his heavy load he was ready to lie down immediately his tummy was full, when had he been willing Rosie would have gone farther afield and to a much later hour. She wouldn't leave George and the Monster would not leave her, and it was seldom they were more than half a mile from camp when Bony went for them in the morning.

116

# The Attack is Switched

Poor old George! Bony decided to give him a holiday and put the Monster to work. How the Monster would react was unknown after so long a period of freedom. In some respects he was behaving perfectly, and so Bony laid him beside the pack saddle which slowly and with care he lifted on to the great hump. The Monster grunted and showed the tip of his uvula, was 'hooshed' at and allowed to twitch himself so that the saddle settled. He did not hug the ground as Rosie did when annoyed, and there was no difficulty in slipping the chest and belly bands under him to clamp the saddle into place. Whilst being loaded his protests were merely half-hearted, and Bony told George how lucky he was.

'If you behave yourself the rest of the day we shall be a happy family,' observed Bony, nudging him to his feet. The warning bell was slung from his neck and he walked behind Old George.

It was a happy family, too, but the next day the Monster behaved erratically. The warning bell stopped, and Bony, turning about, saw that he had broken the nose-line from George's tail and was standing quite still and looking back. He did not want to move when Bony went to him and refastened the line to George's tail, this time more securely.

The same antic happened half an hour later. They were on fairly open country of low ground swells, lightly timbered. Bony could see nothing moving, but was definitely suspicious. Whatever it was he could not scent it as the wind was against it. The other animals were not affected.

117

'I think I'll investigate,' Bony said. 'Down you go.'

Roping one foreleg to prevent him getting up, Bony put down Old George and Rosie, took his rifle and walked back along the Fence. The shadow was no longer over the land. The sky was empty of cloud. The wind was cool and from the south, and Bony went back a mile without seeing anything alive save the eagles high above.

He began the return to his camels on the far side of the Fence, and almost at once found the naked imprints of two aborigines who had been walking in the same direction. He kept with them and found where they had left the Fence and entered a stand of mulgas. They had passed through the trees, had emerged on the far side and gone on away to the west.

The tracks were fresh, and Bony would remember them a year hence. What had been their business? Were they on an innocent walkabout, or were they following Bony and his camels? Had their act of leaving the Fence and entering the trees been dictated by seeing Bony leave his camels to investigate? Their tracks showed they had made no hurried move through the mulga, and to have followed them farther would have achieved nothing, for once knowing they were followed the natives would simply vanish like a mirage.

It was likely that they were Lake Frome aborigines. Bony thought the Quinambie blacks would take longer to make their next move. The incident taken by itself could not be seriously accepted as part of any other scheme to make life unpleasant for the stranger, but it had become obvious that word had gone out that Bony was to be diverted from this investigation. Just how far the natives would go in the matter of direct violence Bony did not know. Bony roused his camels and proceeded southward, not entirely satisfied either way.

The next incident was decidedly more serious. He had retired to his bunk beside the camp fire and was smoking his last cigarette for the day when the clatter of the bell carried by Old George told that this animal had abruptly stood up. They were not more than a quarter-mile from camp and had been lying down for more than an hour. It was now ten o'clock.

Now the bell round a camel's neck is a great recorder of mood and movement. The initiated can tell exactly what the animals are doing. The bell announces when they are feeding, when they are lying down for the night. To Bony it told when Old George was biting the lice on his hide, when he was shifting to throw off worrying ants, when he was getting up and beginning again to feed. All these various actions would be copied by his companions, and finally the bell would tell in which direction they were moving on.

This night the bell clattered when Old George stood up. It then stopped. The ensuing silence indicated that he was standing and merely chewing the cud, but after several minutes during which the bell did not clang

119

there was something obviously peculiar about George just merely standing without movement.

Bony waited for the bell and the bell remained silent. The strap might have broken when the animal stood, or the tongue of the bell might have come adrift. Without the guiding bell, it could be difficult to find the animals the following morning. Not troubling to dress, in his pyjamas, Bony set off to find his camels and the defective bell, taking a spare bell with him.

The night was quiet and dark. The sparse scrub loomed higher than in daylight. He walked circumspectly between the trees in the direction tolled by the now silent bell, and only when he had proceeded half a mile did he decide he must have passed his camels. Then he circled and did this for an hour before giving up and returning to his camp, to rely on tracking them in daylight.

As the day broke he was dressed and sipping a pannikin of tea, and when it was light enough to see the light tracks left by the large and padded feet he followed these tracks to the place where the three camels having fed had lain down for the night. There was no mistaking the marks left by their heavy bodies. Neither was there any misreading of the tracks of a lubra who had advanced to the beasts causing George to stand and ring his bell. The prints of naked feet told a story plainly enough.

The woman doubtlessly had stuffed grass into the bell. She had removed the hobbles from the animals, had mounted one of them and led the remaining two away in a north-easterly direction, for she left no tracks beside those of the camels. Meticulously Bony followed the animals' tracks. He followed them for four miles to where the woman had dismounted, re-hobbled the beasts, and cleared the bell of grass. Her tracks showed that she had departed to the east. Now Bony listened and found he could barely hear the bell away to the north.

The camels were feeding between two timbered sand ridges, a distance from his camp of fully five miles. That was the distance Bony had to tramp back to camp with them for breakfast and then begin the day's work.

The conditions on this Border Fence were harsh enough without having to begin the day with a ten-mile tramp, and no ordinary Australian working man would put up with it. Employment wasn't that scarce. The organizers of this act of sabotage would know that full well, as they would know that repeated doses of the same tactics would surely remove this working man from a locality where he was not wanted.

Who would want him out of it? Who was behind the animosity of the aborigines? For no apparent reason Nugget could want him off the Fence so that he could regain his old section. The lubra who had removed the camels could be that young woman Needle Kent had named as some kind of relative. Nugget's motive was probably obscure, but important enough to him. Then there was Jack Levvey who needed a boss stockman and offered the job. Irritating tactics would not be beyond him. One could go backwards and forwards over these suppositions and get nowhere until these controlled machinations became still more serious and finally disclosed a lead.

The Monster, too, was not happy that day. He kept looking back, his eyes bright with suspicion, till Bony caught his feeling of unrest and wondered if they were being kept under surveillance. There was nothing tangible to confirm the suspicion, but during the afternoon he transferred the saddle and loading from the Monster to Old George and permitted the former to follow without a nose-line. Once, the Monster dawdled far behind, and then caught up with the train as though fearful of being lost. That he was annoyed was evidenced by the manner in which he chewed cud, his jaws moving with almost vicious determination, to have done with it.

However, there was no incident and when Bony camped they seemed content and in good temper. After sundown he freed them in shortened hobbles, and attacked the cooking chores whilst listening to the bell. The dusk gathered and he marked the position where they were feeding.

Later on he made his bunk a short distance from the fire on the clean ground, and then permitted the fire to die down as he squatted beside it and smoked. The evening passed in meditation, and presently the bell clattered to tell him that Old George was lying down for the night. Now he took the nose-lines and unhurriedly walked to where they were resting, approaching with the light wind blowing towards them. Eventually by lying on the ground he could distinguish the shape of their humps against the skyline, and approaching still closer sat with his back against a tree trunk.

*Chapter Thirteen*

# Two Up a Tree

It was a cabbage tree, one of the best to provide shade in summer heat. In shape not unlike an apple tree, its foliage was full and bright green and its branches horizontal and stout. Bony rested against it, but not for long.

It was not any sound, but a feeling of slight chill which arose to settle at the nape of his neck that warned him of danger, that self-same feeling which stiffens a sentinel kangaroo to warn his dozing companions abruptly that all is not right in their world. Bony stiffened and lay full length on the ground to seek skylines. Old George raised his head, and the bell clanged once.

On a skyline rose a pointed object, and the object was moving towards Bony's tree, rapidly becoming larger. Bony bunched his knees, raised his body to stand hard against the tree trunk. Then in the faint starlight the object was about to pass the tree.

Like the old man of the sea Bony jumped on the man's back and planted his hands about the fellow's neck, thumbs at the back. The smell betrayed the aborigine, who emitted a startled shout of fear. The bell clattered and the hobble chains rattled as the camels sprang to their feet, the silence of the night shattered.

The aborigine heaved and twisted, and Bony's thumbs sank into the nerves at the back of the man's head. The victim bent forward, slewed his head, twisted his neck, but the pressure increased, and the fingers tightened about the throat, but not to the point of cutting off breath. The victim remained conscious enough to experience the frightful agony flaring through his brain.

Hobble chains rang like steel on an anvil. Great padded feet thudded upon the ground. A low rumbling roar of diabolic fury ruled the night and the pressure about the aborigine's neck was suddenly released.

'Up the tree!' Bony shouted. 'Fast, you swine. The Monster's on us.'

Instinctively, the aborigine leapt for a branch and swung himself up. Just as actively Bony followed him, certain that the Monster's gaping jaws were but a few inches behind him. The red uvula would be fully extended, and from the mouth half-digested cud would jet. Again came the roar of anger, and this ended in a squeal of frustration. The tree shook as the heavy body pounded the trunk in relentless fury. The branch to which the aborigine and Bony clung shivered and creaked, and both waited for the assault to cease, with the hope that the Monster would fail to uproot the cabbage tree. They could see the Monster's shape as he circled it.

'That,' Bony said, 'is the Lake Frome Monster. Now I know what they say about him is true. But it must have been your tribe who tortured him so that he goes berserk from time to time. I've a mind to knock you off your perch so that you can argue it out with him. I will, too, if you don't talk. What's your name?'

He could see the white of the man's eyes and the glint of white teeth in a mouth grinning with fear. The Monster was moaning, now less angry. It could wait, and would.

'Come on! Who are you?' Bony demanded.

'Quinambie feller. Boss said look for cattle. I was only going home.'

'Liar. Looking for cattle without a horse. Looking for cattle in the middle of the night. How are you called? Out with it, or I'll smash you off the branch.'

'I wasn't doing any harm,' the aborigine almost whimpered.

'No! Only going to move my camels four or five miles. Last night a lubra did it. The Monster likes women but doesn't like aborigines looking for cattle in the dark. I asked you your name.'

The fellow became mute, and Bony reached for a higher branch and stood on the one he had been sitting on. He said:

'I'll kick you off if you don't answer or if you attempt to shift your possie. The Monster's still down there, in case you have forgotten about him!'

The Monster was certainly still below, and he wasn't merely scratching himself against the tree: Old George's bell clanged now and then, telling that he was an interested onlooker.

'Well?' Bony persisted.

'I'm Luke,' replied the aborigine. 'I was out looking for cattle. The boss sent me as I said. I got tossed off me horse when I wasn't thinking, and it was getting late and the horse cleared off from me, the bastard.'

'And you were just walking home?'

'That's right, Ed. You are Ed, ain't you?'

'I am so. Where did you say the horse tossed you?'

'Down south opposite the Number Four Bore.'

The stars said it was past midnight. Had Luke been bucked off his horse at sundown he would have been farther on than Bony's camels and this comforting cabbage tree. More likely than not he would have holed up at dark and waited until break of day before continuing his journey to the homestead. As for the yarn about looking for cattle, it could be checked when next Bony went in for rations.

Time passed slowly and presently the abo balanced himself on his branch to use both hands to roll a cigarette. Leaning against the higher branch, Bony adopted the idea, and when he had consumed the cigarette he thought that the Monster was losing some of his sting. Old George lay down again, and they could hear the soft gurgle as the Monster periodically brought up a mouthful of cud. Now he was leaning hard against the trunk like a drunk against a street verandah post.

The abo made another cigarette, and Bony sat on the branch to see his face when the match was ignited. It was the face of a young man, and it would not be forgotten, nor would his tracks when Bony examined them in the morning. They sat a while in silence before the aborigine said:

'Where did you pick up that mad camel?'

Bony explained the circumstances, adding:

'All he wanted from me was the company of my camels. He's got it, and we've got him.'

'How long do we stay here?'

'Until the Monster becomes hungry and wanders off for a feed. You can then dash off from tree to tree, and heaven help you if he catches you in the open. He can travel faster than a truck: hobbles and all.'

'Why the hell did you bring him this side of the Fence?' complained the aborigine somewhat bitterly.

'To keep lubras and bucks like you from taking my camels at night.'

'I wasn't going to take 'em off. I told you so. How d'you know a lubra took 'em?'

'I can track, stupid. Her feet were bare. It could have been that young lubra with Nugget. I'll know when I see her tracks again.'

Now and then the aborigine eased himself on the branch and the Monster lay down. It was a long night and at last quite peaceful, but every night has an end and when the dawn was advanced the camels did what Bony anticipated they would do.

Old George discovered that his cud was too dry to chew, and thus he stood and began to shuffle in his hobbles to the camp in the hope of a drink of suddy water. The Monster moaned and stood looking at him. He left the tree by a couple of yards and then came back to it in a hurry. Rosie yawned, grunted and stood, and moved off on Old George's tracks. The Monster could not permit himself to be left alone and followed her, and soon all three had disappeared into the scrub.

'Now's our chance,' said the aborigine.

'Better wait a few minutes, then don't forget to look behind you,' Bony advised. 'Meanwhile, tell old Moses and Charlie the Nut from me that moving my camels at night is going to be tough on them. I don't like it, tell them. It annoys me and when I'm annoyed I can be just as rough as the Monster. Now get going, and travel fast.'

'You go to hell,' Luke said, but waited until he had dropped to the ground before he said it. He gazed about cautiously, and then sprinted. Bony jumped down and unlimbered his cramped muscles before going after his camels.

He found them at the camp. Rosie and the Monster were feeding, and Old George was standing with splayed hind legs waiting for his two pannikins of water. The Monster took no notice of Bony. Having washed as best he could with the meagre ration, Bony ate a breakfast of salt beef and hard damper, the last crust of which he took to the Monster.

It ought not to be thought that the camel is an endearing animal, nor can it be said of it that, as the ship of the desert, it is man's closest friend. Like the cat to which it is allied, it cannot be conquered, but like the elephant it can be tamed to undertake certain chores. With patience it can be 'broken' to carry a rider, to work in harness with another to draw a buckboard, to carry a heavy load all day. Not being a utility beast it is best when specialized work is required of it.

The Lake Frome Monster was obviously a beast of burden, but he was a powerful animal where Rosie was light, was older, and was a creature of habit. Bony now needed a steed of stamina. He neck-roped Rosie and Old George each to a tree and put the Monster down beside the riding saddle. The Monster was not amused. He fidgeted, he sniffed at the long iron saddle. He pretended that ants annoyed him and he wanted to stand. Sternly 'hooshed' down, he absurdly attempted to move forward on his knees. So Bony roped him down and forcefully thrust the saddle over his hump and tightened girth and belly band.

The rope binding his bent foreleg then had to be removed, whereupon the Monster attempted to stand and was compelled to lie down. Bony gently placed a foot in the stirrup, and before any weight could be added the camel leapt to its feet in a fraction of a second. You cannot conquer a cat, 'tis said, but you

can partially conquer a camel by wearing him out
before you are worn out.

Bony put him down again, and again put gentle
weight on the nearside stirrup. Thus it went on – up
and down – and before each rebellion the weight of
the man's foot was slightly increased. For the foot to
be caught in the stirrup when that lightning leap upward was made would have meant a broken leg or
lesser injury. Eventually, Bony was able to put all his
weight on the foot and to dance with the free one, and
ultimately he swung the free leg across the saddle and
was seated when the astounded Monster was on his
feet and wondering how he had been tricked.

The Monster laid back his cat ears and attempted
to bite his rider's leg. Bony threatened to kick his teeth
in. Normally polite, Bony called him a dirty brown
bastard. Such epithets as swine, cur, mongrel, etc.,
would have been misplaced as pussy cat. Having won
with patience he waited for the next phase of rebellion,
were such to come, and after five minutes of quiescence
he rolled a cigarette. The Monster looked foolish meanwhile. One of the oldest domesticated animals, the
camel is swift to surrender.

The cigarette consumed, Bony gently jerked the
nose-line to the right, whereupon the Monster turned
in that direction and proceeded without argument.
Back at the cabbage tree where he had perched most
of the night, Bony circled it and picked up Luke's
booted tracks, thus beginning a long day of tracking in
reverse.

Luke had been truthful when he said he had been thrown from his horse. About a mile from where Bony had made his camp, a succession of deep hoof marks in the sand showed that the horse had reared suddenly as if suddenly frightened and then commenced to buck. Luke had obviously been no match for his steed in these circumstances and a larger indentation in the loose sand showed where he had first come to earth in a manner not approved by the Equestrian Association.

Bony recalled that sound travels a long way on a still night and maybe one of the Monster's intermittent bellows on settling down may have been too much for the horse.

Bony, who did not yet trust the Monster sufficiently to dismount, pulled his head sharply round and continued to follow the horse's tracks. These did not lead directly towards Quinambie homestead, but appeared to be tracing a parallel course to the Fence and roughly, as far as Bonaparte could judge, the direction of the section of the Fence which was then cared for by Nugget.

The sun was now high in the sky and Bony began to wish that he had brought his water-bottle. He had expected the horse's tracks to lead him directly to Quinambie, where he had half-hoped to be able to force a showdown with the aborigines. Bone-pointing by stealth having been circumvented, they were obviously still prepared to go to extreme lengths to discourage his further stay in that area. Engrossed in his thoughts he suddenly noticed that the tracks had entered a fairly dense bush of swamp gums and low-growing scrub. Here the tracks were less easy to follow and in a clearing it appeared as if the tracks of Luke's horse had met those of another horse. Bony suddenly pulled his camel to a halt. Just as he did so, there was a sharp 'splat' and the whine of a ricochet as a bullet hit the swamp gum near him a glancing blow and whined off into the distance. Almost simultaneously, Bony heard the sound of the rifle itself.

There was now no question of whether Bony could afford to dismount from the Monster. He flung himself almost headlong from the saddle and darted behind the swamp gum, at the same time reaching inside his shoulder holster for the ·45 revolver which some sixth sense had made him buckle on for the first time earlier that day. There was no sound, except for the Monster, who, enjoying this unexpected freedom, was busily chewing some rough herbage which he had found among the trees, and the occasional bird noises that came from the clump where he was sheltering. Bony cautiously worked his way from tree to tree until he had reached the outside section of the clump. He saw then that maybe a quarter of a mile away was another and a larger bush which extended for perhaps half a mile parallel to the Fence. Obviously, his silent assailant had vanished into this timber. Bony watched for a while but there was no movement and no further shot. He did not believe for a moment that an expert marksman bent on killing him would not have been able to pick up his movements in the timber and be in position for another shot. It seemed obvious that as he had not heeded the previous warnings this was intended to be a sterner one. Bony took it for exactly what it was, a direct and uncompromising threat that if he continued to put his nose into matters concerning Maidstone's murder, he himself would wind up equally dead. Bony kept his revolver in his hand while he worked his way back to where the Monster was still unconcernedly grazing.

Whether the heat of the day had sapped the Monster's capacity for sheer hellishness, Bony did not know. At any rate, he allowed himself to be caught and mounted with the minimum of fuss. Bony cautiously circled round and first followed the tracks which had been made by Luke's horse. Shortly after the meeting with the other horse, and once clear of the belt of trees, they turned directly towards Quinambie Station. Bony followed them for about a mile until this became obvious and then retraced his steps to where Luke's horse had been joined by the other and unknown horse. This was much more interesting. Luke, at best, was only a pawn in this dangerous game someone was playing, and just how dangerous and how high the stakes were Bony had yet to find out.

After the meeting with the other horse, the tracks of the horse ridden by the unknown rider headed directly towards the Fence. Bony followed these tracks, giving a reasonably wide berth to any clump of trees which could shelter a gunman, and after going up a fairly steep rise he suddenly stopped the Monster dead in his tracks. There, not three hundred yards away, was the hut which was Nugget's headquarters for the section of the Fence which he had to patrol! The slab hut appeared to be deserted and only a wisp of smoke coming from the galvanized-iron chimney indicated that it had been recently occupied. There was no sign of Nugget or the lubras and Bonaparte could not see any horse. Bony sat on the Monster in silent thought for a minute and turned and headed slowly back towards his camp.

As he rode thoughts kept jostling themselves in his mind. Nugget – so many things came back to Nugget. Nugget on his own story had been closer than anybody to Maidstone's camp on that vital night. Nugget was a member of the Quinambie tribe of aborigines. Nugget was reputed to have had a Winchester rifle before he acquired his much-talked-about Savage. Nugget could easily have been working in conjunction with the cattle duffers. But motive was the thing. What possible motive could Nugget have had for killing Maidstone? Maidstone did not know him. Even if Maidstone's murder was connected in some way with his photographic activities, the thing just didn't make sense. Even if Nugget had had a record a mile long, there was no danger to him from Maidstone, even if that unfortunate traveller had taken photographs of him from every angle. As he neared his camp, Bony felt mentally weary. There were too many pieces missing from the puzzle.

He was now convinced that Maidstone's death was no accident and that someone had a vital and cogent reason for disposing of him, but so far there was simply no connection between the pieces of the puzzle. Bony had felt up against a brick wall at many times in his previous investigations, but never had he felt so much like a man trying to put a number of little drops of mercury together into a coherent whole. No matter what aspect of the case he touched, the leads seemed to peter out and disappear, just in the very way that the streams and channels in that part of the world mysteriously disappeared underground in the heat of summer. It was a tired and disconsolate detective who fed and watered his camel on his return to camp.

## Chapter Fourteen

# A Glimmer of Light

Bony woke early the next morning. An early-morning breeze was stirring the leaves on the trees round his camp and the chill of the night air still lingered. He brewed himself some hot tea and suddenly put his cup down and gazed unseeingly into the distance. Maidstone! Maidstone had been the man who was killed and the motive for his killing could only be something that Maidstone had seen, or done, or known – something that presented a threat to the man who took his life. Maidstone – he didn't know enough about Maidstone. Certainly Maidstone's actions on his photographic trip had been innocuous enough. It may even have been something that Maidstone did not even realize he knew. The more he thought about it the more Bony was convinced that some at least of the missing parts of the puzzle were centred on Maidstone.

He also thought over his expected reaction to the bullet that had been fired at him. If he said nothing about it, it would confirm in the minds of the aborigines, and anyone else who was doubtful, that he was in fact a policeman; and the web of silence would descend more firmly than ever. If, on the other hand, he was what he outwardly pretended to be, a workman engaged on the Fence, then such an outrage would bring him hot-foot to report to the nearest authority, who in this case would be Newton, and the story would no doubt be relayed to the police. Bony decided that he had to play the part of the outraged civilian who had been the victim of some grossly-negligent target practice and didn't like it. He had to see Newton and he had to see if he could find out something else about Maidstone. He recalled that Maidstone had stayed with Joyce at his homestead and if Joyce would co-operate he proposed to go through every word of any conversation Maidstone had had with Joyce. Somewhere – somehow – there must be something that would give him a lead.

Newton's face was grim as he listened to Bony's story at his headquarters.

'I really didn't think there was very much in this, originally,' he said. 'But now I do. I'll get on to the police at Broken Hill for you and quite frankly I think you need some help. You know this part of the world as well as I do and a man could be knocked on the head and buried here for six months before anybody found him. I don't want to be responsible for that happening to you.'

Bonaparte shook his head :

'No, I've got to play this alone for a while,' he said. 'But I've got an idea that I'm going to need some help shortly. There are a lot of things about this matter that

I don't understand and I think I'll have to get some checking done well away from here if I'm going to find the answers. This is a much bigger thing than a casual crime of a man being killed for money or by some psychopath. I now think there is much more behind all this than I thought originally, and I don't think that all the ends are within this area. My trouble is that I can't afford to step out of character and leave this Fence long enough to set all the inquiries in motion. What I would like you to do is ride out and see me in three days' time, ostensibly to check the Fence, and by that time I hope I may be in a position to tell you that I am ready to have a little checking done and get you to set the wires in motion.'

Newton nodded:

'Well, I'll certainly arrange to do that and if you are nowhere to be found, I suppose you've no objection to me putting the Monster up for auction?'

Bony appreciated the sardonic humour. Newton was a sound fellow and possibly the only one in this desolate area on whom he could rely.

'You might do that,' he said. 'Or you could take him up to the Centre. He should be a great tourist attraction at Ayers Rock. If you could only get him up to the top there he could stand and bellow on moonlight nights and frighten hell out of the tourists. Anyway, so that you won't be worried about me for the next day, I'm off now to see Joyce.

'One more thing,' he said to Newton, as he turned and rode away. 'At this stage of the game I think you had better come and see me in daylight. I am getting rather allergic to people creeping up on me in the night.'

Joyce was hard at work in his office when Bony was announced. He greeted Bony cordially, but with that touch of reserve that Bony had noticed at their first meeting.

'Well,' he said, 'Detective-Inspector, what can I do for you?'

'The first thing,' Bony said, 'is not to call me that while I'm here. Even the walls of Central Australian homesteads have ears, you know.'

'Sorry,' said Joyce. 'Ed, or Ted – Ed, that's your name, isn't it?'

'Yes, Ed it is,' said Bony. 'Since I have seen you I have been the victim of an attempt at black magic, some camel stealing, and I have also been subjected to a little target practice by a marksman who, I think, intended to miss but not by very much.'

Joyce opened his eyes wide:

'The deuce you say,' he said. 'Are you serious?'

'I'm certainly very serious,' said Bony. 'And I'd like you to take it very seriously too, if you would. By that I mean I want your co-operation for an hour, much as I hate to drag you away from these books.'

'Anything I can do to help,' said Joyce.

'What I want to know,' said Bony, 'is this: did Maidstone talk to you very much about himself, or his career when he was here?'

'No, I don't think so,' said Joyce. 'He told me the

usual stuff about him doing this photography business in his spare time and how he'd always been a keen photographer.'

'Did he say anything about what sort of apparatus he had?' said Bony.

'Yes, he showed me his camera,' Joyce returned. 'He was very proud of it. It looked a most expensive and complicated one to me. He had just bought himself a new battery-flash which he hoped to use in getting pictures of cattle and other animals feeding at bore-holes at night.'

'Did he take any pictures round here?' asked Bony.

'He took a few of the homestead,' said Joyce, 'but nothing at night. He said he hadn't yet tried his flash bulbs out. He had just bought himself four dozen of them but hadn't used any.'

'Four dozen,' said Bony. 'Are you sure?'

'Yes,' said Joyce. 'He showed me them. He showed me how the flash worked and I asked him how many he had and he said four dozen.'

Bony thought rapidly. The police report had shown that the inventory of Maidstone's possessions at his camp had shown forty-six flash bulbs. He himself had found the two missing ones, but Maidstone's camera had been empty of film and in the collection of films which the police had developed there were no pictures which had been taken at night. It indeed seemed important that Maidstone had taken pictures at night, and that the film was missing. Bony felt a surge of excitement.

141

'Anything else of any importance you discussed?' Bony asked.

'I can't say what's important and what's not,' said Joyce. 'He told me that he hoped to get some unusual animals, but large station properties in the outback had been so much in the news that he was even prepared to settle for herds of steers drinking at these water holes at night. The Commonwealth Government had apparently been pushing development of the Northern Territory and Western Australia and Maidstone said his magazine was dead-set on running some Central Australian features. Very few people appeared to know anything about the possibility of watering stock by means of bores in areas where water could be found underground and the pictures were to be used to illustrate a story by an expert in this field.'

'Why pick this area?' said Bony. 'Maidstone could surely have had a much more comfortable trip in some of the bore areas of southern Queensland, say round Blackall, or even round Moree in northern New South Wales.'

'Sorry. I can't help,' said Joyce. 'I don't know why he picked this area, he didn't appear to know anybody here either, except that Levvey had asked him to stay if ever he came up this way.'

'What did you say?' said Bony.

'I said Levvey had asked him to stay. He said he had met Levvey in Sydney, New South Wales, shortly after Levvey had got the job as manager on Lake Frome. Levvey had a cottage down at Collaroy or somewhere near that area – Maidstone was on vacation and they'd met at a party.'

Bony suddenly switched the conversation. 'What sort of a station is Lake Frome?' he asked.

'Oh, it's a pretty good place,' said Joyce, 'except that the owners never come here. It's owned by one of these land companies with a lot of shareholders in England, and the place is always run by managers. Still, it's always done quite well.'

'Did you know Levvey before he came here?' Bony said.

'No, I didn't know him at all,' said Joyce. 'The fellow came along one day and introduced himself. Didn't quite expect to see that type of a fellow, but he seemed a good bushman and a good stockman. Couldn't quite imagine what he and Maidstone had had in common at Collaroy. Maidstone seemed an intellectual sort of bloke, interested in photography and all that, and from what I saw of Levvey he hardly appeared to be Maidstone's cup of tea. Still, Maidstone certainly liked the outback life, always got out somewhere for his vacations, and probably Levvey appealed to him as coming from that area. Well, it's time for a drink. Anything else you want from me?'

'No, thanks,' said Bony, and proceeded to talk to Joyce about what he thought of the prospects of developing that area.

'Can't do anything without water,' said Joyce. 'This bore water isn't enough. We need enough to be able to irrigate. If we only had the rainfall we could grow anything here. If you've got enough water and are prepared to put in the fertilizer any sort of soil will grow grass.'

Bonaparte agreed with this theory, and as they sipped their drinks Bony sensed Joyce's very real interest in his adopted country and came to the conclusion that Joyce, as well as Newton, was a man on whom he could rely in a tight spot. While he talked, Bony thought over the information he had got from Joyce. As had happened to him so many times before, the most vital parts of a conversation had never been given to him on his first interview with someone who could possibly help. The really significant things, he reflected, were passed over because they seemed unimportant. It was only the sensational and the dramatic that were ever recounted to him, sometimes with a good deal of embroidery. He reflected how often it paid to talk to a witness again and get out from him all the little bits that he had not thought it worth while mentioning. For the first time since he had come to the Lake Frome area, he began to feel that this would not be the one case from which he had had to retire defeated.

*Chapter Fifteen*

# Time to Wait

Bony's back ached until he was not sure whether it was easier to remain doubled up or to endeavour to straighten it. Whenever he did so, every muscle protested that this was the hardest, most back-breaking section of any marsupial-proof Fence in the whole of Australia. For three days he had fought the debris blown by the wind and watched it blown away over into New South Wales. For three days the wind had set out to make a mockery of his toil. As fast as he pitched one load over, so another one arrived. Even at night the wind whistled and howled through his camp and the camels grunted and stirred uneasily beneath the sting of the sand. The Monster, whose temper was never the best, in particular became restive under the bombardment and at times emitted a bellow of sheer rage at the tormenting of the elements at which he could not strike back. Bony, having lived most of his life in the bush, made himself as comfortable as possible. He was careful to pitch his camp on the lee side of the highest hill he could find and to have his fire on the farthest side so that the smoke blew away from him. Even so, sand was in everything. Sand in the damper, sand in the sugar he put in his tea, sand in his hair – everything tasted of sand. Bony gritted his teeth and wrapped his blankets more securely round him. He began to wonder how many years of his pension he would have given to be sitting in any of the restaurants in Broken Hill looking down at half a roast chicken and a pint of beer. He could have had them at any time during the twenty-four hours in Broken Hill, he thought wryly to himself.

The next day was calmer and by lunch-time some of the stiffness and soreness had been worked out of Bony's back. He had still only gone some three hundred yards from the camp when there was a hail from some distance away and he saw Newton approaching him on his horse.

'Still on it?' said Newton.

'Yes, unfortunately,' gritted Bony. 'As far as I am concerned you can take this damned Fence and if any dingo or wild dog is courageous enough to live in this God-forsaken area, then in my book he deserves to get among the sheep in New South Wales.'

'That's not the right attitude for a pillar of the law,' said Newton.

'Maybe not,' said Bony. 'But it's the right attitude for a man whose back aches the way mine does. Haven't your superiors ever heard of something like a mechanical rake?'

'Can't do that,' said Newton. 'Think of all the men

146

it would put out of work. You wouldn't want to see automation in the outback, would you?'

'Well,' said Bony, 'I've got something for you to do this time, anyway. Come and have a cup of tea and I'll tell you about it.

'Now,' said Bony, when they were both resting with their backs against a convenient cabbage tree near the camp. 'I want you to get this letter to the Superintendent at Broken Hill and I want you to give it into his hands personally. I want no one to know that I am making any inquiries whatsoever outside and if anyone does, I've got an idea that you'll be needing another caretaker for this section of the Fence. Can you find enough work to justify you going into Broken Hill? Could you find some excuse to wait in there for a few days until the replies begin to come through? I trust no one here except you and I can't do any more without the information for which I have asked.'

'Leave it to me,' said Newton. 'A few days in Broken Hill wouldn't do me any harm at all.'

'Right,' said Bony. 'In the meantime, I'll go on being a fairy godmother to this accursed Fence of yours, but please make it back as soon as you can.'

The next few days passed very slowly. Bony schooled himself to wait with as much patience as he possessed. One day he rode in for more supplies but was careful not to discuss anything relating to the matter with anyone whom he met. He was, however, vociferously indignant over people shooting at random and protested most indignantly that he could easily have been killed.

He also said that he thought that some fellow, who ought never to have had a rifle in his hands, shot Maidstone while hunting for something else, and had then been too scared to tell the police about the accident. He was particularly careful on his way back to call on Nugget to tell him that he had had the same sort of experience as Nugget had had himself. He was also careful to tell Nugget that he thought he might take Levvey up on his offer of a job, that he was getting sick and tired of the Fence and that at any tick of the clock he might be down to see Levvey and if Nugget saw him would he let him know.

Nugget looked up sharply from the saddle he was polishing when Bony said this. All effusiveness was wiped from his face and he looked straight at Bony for the first time that morning.

'Yes, that's a good idea,' he said slowly. 'I'd go and see Levvey, he's a good bloke. He'd look after you.'

Just as he was about to leave Nugget, Needle Kent turned up. Bony greeted him cheerily.

'Well, Needle,' he said, 'cattle duffers been keeping you awake again?'

'No,' said Needle viciously. 'And I wouldn't report them if they did. Not to any flaming copper. By the way, I hear you're one.'

'Who on earth told you that?' said Bony.

'Ah, it's all round the camp at Quinambie,' said Needle. 'Why don't you come clean? What's the idea of coming among folks like us pretending you're a workman. No one's going to help the flaming cops

148

round here, particularly if they come dressed up in some fancy dress and do some workman out of a job.'

'You've got me all wrong, mate,' said Bony. 'Whoever's been filling your head with all that rot wants their head read.'

'Maybe I have and maybe I haven't,' said Needle Kent darkly. 'But if you're what I hear you are, I'd hot-foot it back to wherever you came from and put in for immediate leave of absence. The police aren't too popular around this part of the world.'

'Thanks for your advice,' said Bony. 'If it concerned me I'd be grateful for it.'

Bony turned suddenly to Nugget and found that individual watching him very intently with a curious smile on his face.

'By the way, Nugget,' said Bony, 'what did you do with that Winchester rifle you had?'

'Sold it,' said Nugget. 'You don't think I could afford to have two rifles, do you?'

'Ah, don't suppose you could,' said Bony. 'I've got a Winchester myself back home. I don't suppose you've got any of the cartridges left you'd like to sell me?'

'No, I haven't,' said Nugget shortly. 'And it's time I got on strengthening some sections of that Fence. I can't stay gossiping all day, even if you can.'

With that he turned on his heel and said : 'Come on, Needle, I'll talk to you while we are at the Fence.'

Needle growled a 'goodbye' to Bony and catching up Nugget walked on with him.

'Well, Bony,' said that individual to himself, 'I don't

think you'd win any popularity contest round here. The sooner you get this job finished and get out of this place, the better.'

It was just as well that Bony did not know what the next few days were to bring.

## Chapter Sixteen

# Bony Ponders and Needle Acts

Rolled in his blankets by his camp fire that night Bony found it hard to get to sleep. He was well aware of the antipathy with which some sections of a community regard the police and that there are many Needle Kents to whom any authority is an enemy to be out-witted and derided when possible. This did not worry him at all. What did worry him was the human capacity to stand round and watch a policeman trying to make an arrest without feeling in duty bound to come to his assistance. He knew of several cases of policemen being beaten up while trying to arrest a lawbreaker for the benefit of the community while the community itself, or at least a section of it, de-liberately stood by and watched.

Bony lay and gazed up at the stars while he pondered on this perverse attitude of sympathy for the underdog. The police represent to some extent the power of the State; the lawbreaker in some strange way becomes identified with the members of the public and so a crime is none of a person's business unless it begins to affect him directly. Bony well understood the

young untried policeman arresting and charging as
having used 'insulting words' anyone who referred to
him as a 'mug copper'. He also appreciated why some
younger members of the Force could become somewhat cynical about their job and the public generally.
Human nature, however, interested Bony far too much
for him to be a cynic. Analysing his situation he decided that most Australians were innately too fair-
minded to carry this instinctive antagonism towards
the copper too far, even in this remote part of the
outback. He sighed and closed his eyes. All a man
could do was the job he had immediately in front of
him.

This philosophical thought brought him to his immediate superior in Broken Hill. By now the Superintendent would have been relieved, through Newton's
arrival, from the apoplexy which he invariably
suffered during the long silences and absence of reports
to which Bony's individual method of working subjected him. Bony could imagine the Superintendent
inquiring of the heavens as to how he could satisfy his
own superiors on the progress of a case when his
Number One dropped out of sight as completely as the
murderer he was supposedly pursuing. So it was with
a smile of amusement on his lips that Bony at last
dropped off.

The next morning while Bony was preparing to
move out of camp towards the Fence, he was more
than surprised to have Needle ride in leading a camel
carrying bedding, supplies, tools. Needle laid his camel

down and dismounted. He made no reference to his outburst of the previous day.

'Day-ee, Ed.'

'Good-day, Needle,' Bony replied. 'What are you doing here?'

'Had a message from Newton when I got back to camp,' Needle explained in his high-pitched voice. 'Seems the bloke on the section above mine has been carted off, appendix or something, and Newton says to get you to come along and help. Wants us to spend a couple of days tidying up that bit of the Fence.'

Bony thought rapidly. He did not believe Needle. Newton had mentioned nothing of this to him and Bony could not imagine that the overseer would have him taken away from this area where he knew things were likely to start opening up interestingly. On the other hand, if he refused to go it would not only reveal his suspicions of Needle but give confirmation of the theory buzzing along the Fence that he was a police officer in disguise. As the workman he was *pro tem.*, he could have no legitimate reason for disobeying what appeared to be a direct message from Newton. At the same time he had to take into account that should Needle be mixed up in the murder, perhaps even being one of the cattle duffers, the real basis for his visit could be an attempt not only to remove 'Ed Bonnay' from this section, but to remove him permanently at some convenient place and time. He decided he had to take the risk of accompanying Needle:

'Right, Needle. I'll pack up and get me gear together. What about tools?'

'No need for 'em,' said Needle. 'I've got some rakes and an axe for any posts we have to cut. Better bring some grub for a couple of days though, and some blankets.'

Bony loaded the Monster with these items and watered George and Rosie, whom he left grazing near the camp site.

'Exactly where are we going?' he asked as they set off.

'About twenty miles north of the gate in the Fence near Bore Ten. Take us a good half-day. We'll follow the Fence on the eastern side.'

After they had passed the gate in the Fence near Bore Ten Needle seemed to become more affable:

'Reckon I'll be gettin' south on leave soon. You know, a bloke gets pretty edgy up here. Sorry I spoke the way I did yesterday.'

'No offence taken,' said Bony. 'It's natural not to want people snooping about. But when you picked on me you chose the wrong fellow.'

'Newton said we'd better take stock and see what fencin' material this bloke's got in hand. Talkin' about stock,' said Needle, 'did I ever tell you about a cousin of mine who drove the flamin' nightcart up in a little country town in north New South Wales?'

'No, I don't think you did,' said Bony.

'Well,' said Needle with a chuckle, 'this was a little place with no sewerage. Me cousin had the game sewn

154

up. As well as collectin' the pans he picked up the garbage cans, had a cart fitted up for the purpose pulled by an old grey mare. The old girl used to go along from house to house, stopped at the right places and waited for him. She knew the round better than he did. Me cousin never had to say a word, she was such a quiet old thing. Anyway, one day the mare took fright, no one ever knew why, and cleared off down the street, and you can guess what happened. Doors flew open, pans fell out in the road, lids came off – what a stinkin' mess! Anyway, me cousin caught the mare, tied her to a post, got a shovel and went back and tried to clean the stuff up. Shovelling it back into the pans he was when a nosey old dame comes along and says: "I see, my good man, you had an accident."

' "Accident be blowed," said me cousin. "What makes you think that? Ain't had no accident. I'm only stocktakin'! " '

Bony laughed agreeably. 'What were you doing before you worked on the Fence, Needle?'

'Shearin'. Out between Warren and Bourke. Times I've been so scratched with burrs from hand to elbow you couldn't have seen me skin. Good money, but thought I'd move on before I was torn to shreds.'

'Did you ever work on a cattle station?' Bony asked.

'Yes. I can do anything on the land. You name it, I've done it.'

Bony tucked away the piece of information that Needle would certainly know something about stock.

They stopped for a brew of tea and some food

beneath the shelter of a mulga clump and now Needle appeared in no hurry at all to press on. He smoked and talked while Bony grew increasingly distrustful of this sudden affability and increasingly concerned that he was getting farther away from the area where he felt he should be. Eventually, after a third cup of tea Needle announced there was only another hour's ride to go, so they'd best get on with it.

At three o'clock he declared they had reached the place in the Fence where they were to start the cleaning-up process, working for some five miles north, watching for loose wires and broken posts and cleaning away any debris from the base of the Fence. During the afternoon two posts had to be renewed and by sundown they had covered only two miles of the section.

After hobbling the camels for the night the men made another brew of tea over the camp fire and got more beef and damper from the tucker box.

'With an early start should think we'll finish the section easily tomorrow. I'm turnin' in.' Rolling himself in his blanket Needle stretched out near the fire. Bony also wrapped himself in a blanket but he remained upright, his back against a cabbage tree. He was going to make sure Needle was well asleep before he himself dozed off. As the cherry-red embers glowed he gazed thoughtfully into them and wondered about Needle's motive in being so genial all of a sudden, completely antagonistic one day, co-operative and companionable the next. If it made sense it was that for some important reason Needle had deliberately lured him away from his camp.

Bony rolled and lit one of his abominable cigarettes and smoked it, waiting to see if Needle's sleep was genuine. After a while an irresistible drowsiness came over Bony himself. He stood up and walked round the fire and threw some more sticks on. Needle did not stir. His breathing appeared to be coming regularly and evenly, but Bony listened to it for some time before he went back to his tree and settled against the trunk. He decided not to sleep at all, but after a while the inevitable happened. He was physically weary after a day of riding and working along the Fence and he dozed off.

He woke with a start. The ashes in the camp fire were cold. The first light of dawning was chill and grey and he knew something was wrong. He looked over to where Needle had stretched out for the night, but Needle was gone, his riding camel as well. The pack camel with the gear was still hobbled with the Monster near by. Inspector Napoleon Bonaparte rose and heartily cursed his propensity for sleeping deeply once he went off.

He got the camels together and made his way back along the Fence as quickly as he could. He passed his own camp site without having seen any sign of Needle Kent and kept going with the idea that he might find Needle at Nugget's shanty if his companion of the day before had not given himself too good a start.

When he got to the gate near Bore Ten Bony dismounted, and, looking for tracks, walked carefully along the other side of the Fence. Needle might have passed through the gate. If he had there were no signs of it. But there were tracks – of a single horse – and of something else; something that made Bony curse beneath his breath: more tracks, of a considerable number of cattle. And as Bony followed them up the Fence he saw the occasional dropping which verified that the tracks were fresh.

He now had proof that his presence round this area must have been most inconvenient for the cattle duffers. While he was about they had been unable to do anything about moving cattle as they could not know exactly where he would be at any particular time. Either Needle was one of the cattle duffers and had lured him away for the purpose of having more cattle moved, or he had been paid to do the job of transferring Ed Bonnay to a certain fixed site temporarily. As Bony had suspected when he had allowed himself to be carried off, there was a very good reason for Needle changing his ideas so quickly.

Nugget and his wife and children were near their untidy shanty when Bony arrived.

'Good day, Nugget. Seen Needle?' he asked.

'No. Ain't seen me sister, either, not since this morning that is. If that crazy beanstalk's gone off with her I'll stop his clock, too right I will.'

Bony hesitated briefly. It would seem more natural to tell Nugget of the previous night's happenings than to conceal them.

'I was out with Needle doin' some work on the

Fence and he just lit out; vamoosed. Woke up this morning and he was gone. No note, no nothing,' he said.

Nugget laughed, though not with his customary mirth.

'Wonder he didn't cut your throat before he left, the way he hates policemen. You're lucky he only disappeared. But if I catch me sister with him I'll make the bastard wish he was a goner for good.'

Bony decided it was best to ignore Nugget's persisting reference to policemen. His indignation was obviously assumed and he probably knew exactly where both Needle and his sister were, but it was equally obvious that no amount of questioning would ever get that out of him. Moreover, Bony was not in a position where he could risk asking many questions at all.

'Well, beats me,' he said. 'Nothing I can do. I'll just have to wait until Newton gets back and let him know what's happened.'

'Yeah. That's it,' said Nugget. 'Maybe he's gone up to join old Looney Pete.' He gave his mirthless laugh again.

'I'll work close to my camp today,' Bony said, 'in case he does show up. If Newton comes down tomorrow would you tell him I want to see him?' He had no intention of disclosing that he knew Newton was away.

'He's not likely to be down tomorrow,' said Nugget. 'But if I see him I'll tell him.'

'Thanks,' said Bony and turned away.

'By the way,' he turned after going a few yards. 'Quinambie must have been shifting some cattle down. Do they bring them out this way when they sell 'em?'

'What d'ya mean?' said Nugget.

'There are tracks along the Fence,' said Bony.

'Could be,' said Nugget shortly. 'They're always changin' cattle around at these stations.'

Bony was certain the tracks were those of stolen beasts. What other motive could Needle possibly have had in getting him away from the area. Crazy or not Needle was in on the cattle duffing, if not the murder, up to his neck.

The following morning Bony had another visitor. This place was getting like the Hill, so many people gadding about. And this caller was most unexpected. It was Commander Joyce from Quinambie Station, alone and riding a horse, his riding gear immaculate, even to cravat. But Joyce was a very worried man.

'I can see I've had my head in the clouds for a long time. I didn't really believe there was any cattle rustling going on. But now I know for myself I thought I should come and tell you immediately. I had about one hundred and fifty head in one of my paddocks – in prime condition – about ready to send off. Yesterday I took an unexpected buyer out and they just weren't there. Haven't told anybody else about this. You're the first to know . . . er . . . Bonnay. Can't afford this sort of thing. What can you do about it?'

The Commander's back was up now that he'd been pricked.

Bony spoke bluntly. 'It is vital we keep them guessing. Go back to your station and say nothing to anybody, least of all to your overseer. And particularly if you see Nugget or Needle Kent say nothing to them about this whatsoever. If you need any explanation for coming out to see me say you brought a message from Fred Newton via your pedal radio that he wouldn't be able to make his usual inspection this week. You know nothing about your cattle, not even how many head you have. And you haven't missed any. Have you a clear picture?'

Joyce sat his horse looking down at Bony, respect mingling with righteous anger in his glance. 'Yes, I've got it. But I hope you've got it too. Do you know how much one hundred and fifty cattle are worth?'

Bony's voice was charming and polite. 'I know exactly,' he said. 'And I've been pushed around by my Superintendent, attacked by your natives, had the bone pointed at me, been shot at, had to let myself be made a fool of; and above all I'm doing hard labour in the stress of heat, sand and flies on this accursed Fence. All the same I retain a very personal interest in the whole of this case I have consented to take up. That is why I am here. Don't worry, Commander. No one is going to get away with your cattle or anything else. I give you my word.' And with this Joyce had to ride away content.

*Chapter Seventeen*

# Bony Pays a Visit

For a day or so after Joyce's visit Bony felt elated. Following Needle's action, which had been transparent to the point of desperation, Joyce's news sorted out the pieces of the puzzle further so that they were beginning to fall into place neatly. Time was running out for the cattle duffers, if not for Maidstone's killer, and Fred Newton, Bony felt sure, would bring back from the Hill the remaining information he needed to act authoritatively.

A week later, however, Bony was beginning to give Newton up for lost, resigning himself to a prolonged if not lifelong sentence of toil on the Fence. As one day followed another and he raked and heaved buckbush over the net he mentally compared his lot with that of the innocent but convicted prisoners he had seen suffering on Devil's Island on one of those rare occasions his wife had dragged him to a cinema. When his thoughts were blackest Newton rode into camp accompanied by a stranger.

'Your Superintendent wouldn't trust me to deliver those reports you asked for,' drawled the overseer with a grin for Bony's look. 'He's brought this character up specially from Sydney to act as mailman.'

'Detective-Inspector Wells, C.I.B.,' the character introduced himself. 'Always wanted to meet the fabulous Napoleon Bonaparte. The C.I.B. got very excited when the information you asked for began to come through. It appears that a lot of vague rumours have been reaching them and this request of yours hit them right where it helped them add up two and two. They sent me out pronto to Broken Hill, wouldn't trust the gen through the post or on the wire, so here I am to give it to you.'

'I can see I'm not going to be let in on anything,' complained Newton good-humouredly as the two men kept their counsel in front of him.

'Your assumption is correct,' said Bony. 'However, one piece of information I will pass on to you, pal. You need a replacement for Needle. He's done a bunk, although I have a fair idea where I might be able to find the rascal should I find it necessary to snaffle him.' Bony brought the overseer up to date with events on the Fence while he and Wells listened intently.

'Well, I'll be damned!' exclaimed Newton. 'What next!'

Bony accepted the overseer's remark literally. 'What I suggest you do,' he said with a smile, 'is prepare us a meal while Wells and I go for a little walkabout along the net. I can show him the kind of torture you've been inflicting on a member of Her Majesty's Forces for the past month.'

'I'll be damned!' Newton said again. 'And who do you think is overseer round here? All right. I'll do it for you this once.' He threw a few sticks on the fire. 'But I warn you,' he observed to the departing figures, 'if there's anything doin' on the detection front I'm entitled to be first in the know, don't forget.'

Bony and Wells strolled off and when they came to an open stretch of the Fence where anyone approaching could be seen for several miles from all sides Wells handed Bony the reports he had brought with him from New South Wales. Bony squatted on his heels and read the papers carefully. Then he looked up at Wells with a gleam of satisfaction in the blue of his eyes as he handed them back. 'That's it, the missing piece. That must be it.'

'Headquarters certainly think so,' said Wells. 'What's the next move in your opinion, Bonaparte?'

Bony, still on his heels, looked as if he could rest there comfortably till the end of time. 'The first thing I propose to do,' he said meditatively, 'is to hand in my resignation to Newton. The second, I'm going down to Levvey to see about that job he offered me. There is no doubt in my mind now that it is at Lake Frome Station rather than at Quinambie or along the Fence that the person I have become interested in will have to show his hand. I also propose to see that the necessary publicity is given to my intentions so that anyone with an interest in what I might uncover will be drawn as by a magnet to the spot. But in the meantime I can't afford to be seen hanging about like this.'

Abruptly he stood up. 'Now,' he said to the attentive Wells, 'this is what I want you to do.'

When they got back to camp Wells announced that he would leave immediately after the meal and suggested it would be best for Bony if Newton left too. 'Any company seen about at this stage could queer the whole pitch, and especially if anyone sees me with you,' Wells farewelled Bony. 'They'd certainly tumble to it that I am one of your higher-ups.'

'Right,' Bony agreed.

Newton looked up quizzically as he finished off his tea. 'No use askin' what all the mystery is about yet?'

'No use at all,' said Bony cheerfully as both visitors mounted their horses. 'But I take pleasure now in the presence of this witness in telling you that as of this instant one Ed Bonnay is resigning from his exalted position as caretaker of one section of this blasted Fence. I'm sorry to give you such short notice, but on the credit side, I'm not asking for a reference.'

'You wouldn't get one anyway,' growled Newton, 'leaving me in the lurch like this. What if we get another westerly?'

'Cheer up,' said Bony, 'all will resolve itself satisfactorily in the end. Tell you what, Fred. Let us meet in Broken Hill for a beer when it is all over and I will let you have the full story then.'

He watched the two men ride off. He was conscious of being very much an isolated man again and he felt confident that there was much to be done and plenty more risks to be taken before he brought this case as he hoped he soon would to the proper conclusion of an arrest.

The next day Bony called on Nugget.

'Well, I've chucked my job,' he said. 'Can't stand that blasted Fence a minute longer. Needle leaving me like a shag on a rock was the last straw. It's too damn lonely for me.'

'Good idea, Ed,' said Nugget. 'I don't know how you stuck it so long; that's the worst section of the Fence. A bloke like you oughtn't to be doing that.'

Nugget seemed in a high good-humour.

'Yeah, it's not much of a job,' said Bony, 'and the pay's not wonderful either. Think I'll mosey along on Sunday night and see Levvey. Reckon he'll be home at that time?'

'Oh, I don't know,' said Nugget. 'Don't know much about his movements. Why don't you get Joyce to call up the station on the wireless and tell him you'll be down.'

'Good idea – I might do that,' said Bony. 'By the way,' he asked, 'I don't suppose Needle has turned up?'

'Not a sign of him,' returned Nugget.

'Well, so long, Nugget, see you around.'

'Bye,' said Nugget.

Bony then called on Joyce. 'Your wireless still functioning?' he asked.

'Yes,' said Joyce. 'Any message you want passed on?'

'Wonder if you would do me a favour?' Bony said.

'Would you call Lake Frome Station at nine o'clock to-night and tell them I'll be down Sunday and hope to see Levvey. I've chucked my job on the Fence and I hear he is looking for a stockman.'

All this in a loud voice which Bony hoped would carry to other members of the homestead, and, in particular, to Luke, whom he had noticed busily engaged in washing down the station utility not very far from where he and Joyce were standing. As Joyce walked to the gate with him, Bony said to him in a low voice:

'And not another word about anything – understand?'

'All right by me,' said Joyce. 'Just what you've told me to say and no more?'

'Just that,' said Bony.

Bony decided that the Monster was the ideal companion for his trip to Lake Frome Station. This was apparently the country, if any, which the Monster regarded as his home. Certainly it pursued a steady gait, and after crossing the Fence and passing the silver sheen of Bore Ten in the afternoon sun, seemed quite tireless as it rolled along the plain country. Bony was careful to keep well clear of all clumps of trees and to keep to the middle of the open country. He was alert for the slightest movement that threatened danger; but all seemed peaceful. It was important, he thought wryly, at least to have the opportunity of putting his theory to the test.

It was also important to Bony that he should not

arrive at the homestead in daylight and that the homestead should know that he was coming. That was why he had mentioned it to the people he thought most likely to spread the news to everyone who could have been remotely connected with the strange events of the last two months, and that was why, as he drew nearer to his destination, a sudden chill of apprehension made him wonder whether he was right, or whether he was about to make the greatest fool of himself of all time. Always on the eve of the winding-up of one of his cases, Bony felt this strange disquiet. Gnawing feelings of doubt and uncertainty as to his own reasoning processes possessed him. These, he knew, disappeared immediately it was time to stop thinking and start acting. The long periods of silent plodding investigation, the days and nights of relative inactivity, would only be worth while if he was right. If he was wrong, this would be a blunder which could ruin his career.

These reflections were brought to an abrupt end as the outbuildings of Lake Frome homestead loomed up in the distance in the gathering dusk. There were lights in the homestead as Bony approached it. He was more careful than ever now. He listened to every sound. The Monster was now showing distinct signs of nervousness. Twice he stopped dead and had to be coaxed and finally kicked into going on, a procedure to which that animal made considerable objection. Bony was surprised to see that there were no cattle in the yards and he then recalled that he had seen hardly any cattle in the fifty-mile ride from Bore Ten to the homestead. This struck him as being particularly unusual. He was very thoughtful as he tied the Monster to a post.

Bony, as is the way in the outback, went to the back door, which in Lake Frome homestead opened directly into the kitchen. He knocked. The door was opened by Levvey and from the appearance of the kitchen table Bony saw that Levvey and his wife had just been having a meal.

'Oh, hullo, Ed,' he said. 'Come in. You go inside for a while,' he said to his wife. 'I want to talk business to Ed.'

'Thanks, Mr Levvey,' said Bony. 'I've come about that job you offered me. I've quit my job on the Fence.'

Levvey looked at him. Suddenly he went to the door his wife had gone through and turned a key in the lock. 'Don't want to be interrupted,' he excused himself. 'Wife gets pretty nosey at times. Can't let 'er know all me business. If she knows the whole tribe knows.'

'Sure,' said Bony, 'I understand. Well, like I said, I'm after work. I can handle stock. There's only one thing, if Needle Kent is here I won't work with him. The bastard left me properly in the lurch on the Fence.'

'Did he now?' said Levvey. 'And have you got any more theories about that fellow Maidstone you were talking to me about?'

'Well, I have a few,' said Bony. 'You know, a bloke doesn't get much to do lying out under the stars except think, so I've been thinking about these cattle duffers. I think that Maidstone was at Bore Ten at the same time as the cattle duffers went to water the stock, or maybe their horses,' he said. 'I think also, that Maidstone took a couple of flashlight photographs of those horses when they were drinking and probably the blokes sitting on them and I think that somebody didn't like being photographed and proceeded to put a bullet through Mr Maidstone.'

Levvey's eyes narrowed.

'That's a very interesting theory, Ed,' he said. 'Seems to me for a Fence worker, you've been taking a great interest in this Maidstone fellow and what happened to him. I also hear through the grapevine the blacks at Quinambie think you are a policeman. What would you say about that, Ed?'

Bony leaned back in his chair, yawned and stretched his hands above his head. In the process he looked at his watch. He answered the question obliquely :

'I don't know that I'm much of a policeman, Mr Levvey,' he said. 'Sometimes I can't see things when they're right under my nose. You've been asking me a lot of questions, let me ask you one for a change. How long have you been managing Lake Frome Station?'

'Don't know that it's any of your business, Ed,' said Levvey, 'but I've been up here for six months. What I'd like to know is why, if you are a copper, and I think you are one, why should you come and ask me for a job?'

'Oh, well,' said Bony, 'I knew Maidstone back

round Sydney and he told me he was a cobber of yours and I thought I would like to come and see how you were getting on.'

There was a dead silence in the room.

'Just what do you mean by that, Ed?' said Levvey. He rose slowly from his chair as he spoke.

'Just this,' said Bony. 'That when Joyce rang up to let you know that Maidstone was coming to Lake Frome Station to visit you at your invitation, it seemed rather a peculiar repayment of the hospitality he had given you at Collaroy to send someone out to put a bullet through him.

'Oh, no you don't,' said Bony, as Levvey reached for a rifle standing in the corner of the kitchen. He pulled out his revolver as he spoke.

'Now you just sit down there, Mr Levvey, and we'll continue this interesting little talk.'

'I don't think you'll be continuing it long,' said Levvey. 'Have a look behind you.'

'That's a very old trick,' said Bony, 'and personally I've never fallen for it.'

'Well, you'd better fall for it this time, you smart Alick cop!' snarled a voice behind him.

It was Nugget's voice. 'Better drop that revolver,' he continued, 'it won't do you any good. You see, I got a Winchester, after all.'

Bony slowly dropped his pistol on to the floor and raised his hands.

'Well, you certainly set it up for me,' he said.

'We set it up for you, all right,' sneered Levvey.

171

'And you fell for it. We'll even take you out and show you where the real Jack Levvey is buried and maybe we'll have another little grave alongside that one. Maybe we might put up a little cross to the memory of a cop who thought he was smart.'

'I still don't see how you worked it,' said Bony. 'I suppose you and Nugget were in this cattle-duffing business together?'

'You're quite right,' said Levvey. 'Nobody's going to hang round the centre of Australia for a few lousy pounds a week. We can sell beef cattle anywhere at twenty pounds a head and no questions asked. There were three hundred head in the last two lots we passed through here. Three hundred head at twenty pounds a head – just work that one out! We only had to keep the game going for another few months then we could disappear and leave everyone to try and figure out the answers.'

'How did you get rid of Levvey?' said Bonaparte.

'He met with an accident on the way in,' said Nugget. 'Maybe someone was out shooting kangaroos and accidently shot him.'

'You're quite wrong about me sending somebody out to shoot Maidstone,' said the man who called himself Levvey. 'Maidstone just shot himself. Sure he took photographs of Nugget and me watering our horses, but that wouldn't have mattered, but he had to go on and shoot his big mouth off when I introduced myself as Levvey. He said, "You're not Levvey, I met Levvey down at Collaroy" – he left us no option but to kill him,

172

and with you out of the way there's nobody going to know anything. Besides we won't be here much longer.'

'Was anybody else in this with you?' asked Bony. 'What about Needle Kent?'

'That's the final and last question,' said the so-called Levvey. 'We haven't got all night. The answer's no — it's a two-way split, mister. Needle had had a belly-full of working on the Fence and he got paid a few quid to get you out of the road. Besides, he'd like to be a member of Nugget's family. Nugget told him it was a joke on a mug copper. No, Nugget and I worked this out and Nugget got the job on the Fence to be handy on the spot. He has all the pull with the abos. He comes from the tribe. We decided that whoever the next manager was, no one would expect anyone here to know him and we would be safe for the six months before I was expected to go south on leave or send in detailed reports. It's a two-way split, except that Nugget here, he likes rifles and does all the shooting. Now he's going to have a little more practice, aren't you, Nugget?'

'You'll only make things worse for yourselves. You know you can't get away with this.'

'We don't have to get away with it for very long. Just one more clean-up and we will be on our way.'

Something had gone wrong. Bony was now fighting for time.

'Suppose you think it over before you do anything you regret. Killing a policeman will make sure you will be extradited, even if you get out of the country.'

'Don't worry about us,' said Levvey, with sardonic humour. 'They'll have to find us first.'

Bony supposed he had been in tighter spots but he couldn't at the moment remember when. In his eagerness to get the evidence he had overlooked the propensity for even the best-laid plans to go awry.

'Come on – out!' said Nugget roughly to Bony.

Bony walked outside, followed by Nugget and Levvey, but some twenty yards outside the kitchen door he halted, as if uncertain which way to go.

'Keep moving,' said Nugget, digging the rifle savagely into Bony's back.

Then everything seemed to happen at once. Bony took a severe but glancing blow on his left shoulder and was flung forward to the ground. Nugget who was immediately behind him took the full brunt of it and was dashed to earth with a sickening thud. The rifle flew wide. It was not until Bony raised himself on his hands and saw in the light from the open kitchen door Levvey dashing for that room, with a large and bellowing mass in hot pursuit, that he realized what had happened. The Monster had either not been tethered properly or had somehow worked himself loose and had gone completely berserk. Squealing with rage, neck outstretched, jaws gaping wide, uvula fully extended, he was now firmly charging the doorway through which Levvey had fled.

Bony felt firm hands lift him to his feet.

'Sorry we're late,' said Wells. 'Got off the road into a sand drift. What on earth is going on?'

174

'Quick,' said Bony. 'Get Nugget, and into the front of the house.'

Two constables emerged out of the darkness and grabbed the barely conscious Nugget and raised him to his feet.

Pushing Nugget in front, the party made for the front of the homestead. A badly frightened Mrs Levvey was crouched in the hall.

'Stay here with Nugget and Mrs Levvey,' Bony ordered the constables.

He and Wells found their way to the inside kitchen door. It was still locked but it couldn't withstand the combined charge of Bony and Wells. A most amazing sight met their eyes. Levvey was standing behind a dresser, still so bereft of thought by the sudden emergency that he had not even looked for his key. The Monster, with shoulders wedged in the door frame as far as they could go, had managed to reach the table and was calmly eating half a loaf of bread which had been left from supper.

It was not until Levvey and Nugget were hand-cuffed and the Monster secured in a horse stall beyond hope of breaking loose that Bony remembered his sense of grievance.

'You were late,' he accused Wells. 'You nearly made it just in time for the funeral.'

Wells looked worried. 'I tried to explain,' he said, 'out there. The track in was badly defined and we got off it and well and truly bogged in loose sand. Had to do the last few miles on foot.'

Bony looked at him. 'Then that was the rumble I heard, of six pairs of policeman's boots. I thought it was thunder.'

Wells grinned, visibly relieved. Bony was going to take it well after all.

Bony turned to the constable who entered the room.

'Levvey and Nugget are to be guarded all the time,' he said. 'I don't trust the natives round here. We'll take shifts. We'll stay the night here and leave early in the morning.'

'Yes, sir,' said the constable. 'When am I to go out and shoot that camel?'

'When are you going to do what?' asked Bony.

'Shoot the camel,' said the constable.

For once Bony appeared to be speechless and Wells intervened. 'I told the Superintendent about it,' he said. 'He'd heard the stories, including the one you told me about you and Luke being treed. He said to tell you it was a menace and to destroy it.'

'That camel could have saved my life and probably did. The Superintendent can come and shoot it himself if he wants to!'

Wells and the constable exchanged glances. Bony caught a look of warning on Wells's face.

'He will be safe until morning, anyway,' said Wells. 'You'd better come and get some rest. I'll take the first shift with the prisoners.'

Shortly before dawn, Bony woke. His mind went back over the events of the night before. Suddenly he pulled on his boots and went outside. When the constable called him at six a.m. he was back and apparently asleep.

After breakfast they made ready for departure. The utility was retrieved by one of the constables and some hands from the station, and Wells waited to see that Bony was occupied and said something to the other constable, who went out with a rifle. In a moment he ran back at the double.

'That camel,' he cried. 'It's gone. The gate of the yard is open and there's no sign of it.'

'That's funny,' said Bony. 'One of the station natives must have let it out.'

'Yes,' said Wells, looking hard at Bony. 'And no doubt the Superintendent will be interested to know what I think really happened.'

'Oh, I don't know,' said Bony. 'I don't know why you should worry him, particularly when I wasn't going to mention how you nearly involved the Department in having to pay superannuation to my widow!'

## Chapter Eighteen

# Reflections

It was three weeks later in Broken Hill when Bony met Newton for the last time. Levvey and Nugget had both been charged with murder and remanded in custody without bail. They were awaiting the visit of the Supreme Court Circuit Court for trial.

Needle Kent's part in the affair had, Bony felt sure, been confined to the one episode when he was led away from the Fence, and beyond reporting the bare facts to his Superintendent, Bony left it to the Department to pursue him or otherwise as it thought fit. So far no instructions had been received, and Bony guessed that the exact nature of the offence committed by Needle would puzzle the experts, as at the time he, Bony, was emphatically claiming not to be a policeman.

The ultimate destination of most of the stolen cattle had been traced and the purchasers of those which had not been slaughtered had been surprised to learn that they could gain no title to stolen goods – even cattle. Joyce had arranged for the sale of these cattle on the spot, rather than have them returned to Quinambie, but before his trip south for this purpose, he and Bony had had a short sharp interview with Moses and the males of his tribe. The Quinambie blacks had hastily departed for regions unknown.

Bony had thought of charging Luke and Charlie the Nut as accessories to the murder of Maidstone, but had decided against it. Inquiries had shown that Nugget had bought the co-operation of the tribe by keeping them well supplied with tobacco, rifles and cash which they could spend on the Syrian. Nugget was too cunning to supply the tribe with liquor, for he knew that this would have led to complaints and would have brought the Aborigines Welfare Board and the police to this area. It appeared also that Nugget was, in fact, old Moses's son-in-law and it was obvious that the attacks on Bony had been made at Nugget's direct instigation.

Bony couldn't help but feel sorry for these nomads in a changing world, when the way of life of the white man had meant that the lands over which once they hunted and roamed at will had been fenced and reduced to private ownership. From hunting their own food the aborigines had been brought down to relying on white men who largely despised them. The rapidly changing world had made their young men restless with the old customs without being able to follow those of the new civilization. Quite apart from his feeling of kinship with them, Bony realized just how little chance most of them had of ever receiving the education which could bring them out of their precarious no-man's-land into the white man's world.

Newton ordered two glasses of beer and led Bony over to a table in a secluded corner of the hotel lounge where the two men had met up for a chat. 'Now,' he said. 'Quite apart from my natural curiosity, you sure owe me something for letting an inexperienced labourer look after one of the most important sections of my Fence. Whether I'll ever get 'er back in proper shape or not I just wouldn't know. I want the whole story.'

'Well,' said Bony, 'I shouldn't talk to you until after the trial, but I really do owe you something. However, you must forget what I tell you, as all this still has to be proved.

'The whole story started when Levvey, whose real name, by the way, is Graham, and who had been suspected of stealing stock in the Riverina in New South Wales, just disappeared from the records of the New South Wales police and from that State. He had, in fact, decided to hole up in Central Australia. He had also worked out that the best way of losing himself was to live with a tribe of blacks. Finally, he chose those who later became known as the Quinambie tribe. He took a lubra from among the native women and had actually lived with the tribe for some time before they moved to Quinambie. It was while he was living with the tribe that he first met Nugget.

'Nugget knew all about Lake Frome Station, for he had been an itinerant worker on stations round about most of his life. He also knew about Joyce's reputation for inexperience with his cattle. Nugget told Levvey of the isolation of Lake Frome and he made inquiries and found that the manager there was largely left to his own devices. It was not long before he began to see the makings of a racket on a very large scale.'

Newton broke in: 'Levvey – sorry – Graham must have been a beaut organizer,' he said. 'He certainly prepared the way very carefully.'

'Yes,' said Bony. 'Let's call him Levvey. It's simpler. One of the ways was to take advantage of the presence of the Lake Frome Monster to make the area sound extremely unhealthy for any nomads other than the blacks whom he wanted about him and whom he could trust. The fewer people who came near Lake Frome the better. So the legend of the Monster was magnified to the point where natives from any other tribe would not dare visit the area and even the few white travellers proceeded with caution.'

'It was surely a pretty long shot,' Newton objected. 'How on earth would he think he could get away with holdin' himself out as a manager?'

'You must realize,' said Bony, 'that nobody knew the new manager; and Levvey knew enough about stock and station life to pull it off. Unfortunately, there was no way of getting the new manager out of the way except by killing him and Nugget had no compunction about doing this. Levvey simply arranged to appear at the same time and introduced himself as the new manager. Before this happened, the Quinambie blacks had already moved into Joyce's property and gradually became accepted. Nugget had managed to get a job on the Fence and after Levvey arrived, apparently not having known any of them before, the game was on. It obviously couldn't last, for soon someone would have made inquiries about the absence of word from the real Levvey, but as luck would have it he was not married, and had no close relatives. As far as the station was concerned, Levvey typed short reports well enough following on the pattern of the ones he found in the office to allay the suspicions of his employers for the time being.

'It was unfortunate for Eric Maidstone that he had to visit the part of the world where the real Levvey had told him he was going. The wireless message which Levvey received must have been a bombshell to him. Maidstone had not only met the real Levvey, but he was actually on his way to Lake Frome homestead. Levvey and Nugget decided that the best thing was to be absent from the homestead and arranged to round up some more of Joyce's cattle at a time when they thought that Maidstone would already have passed Bore Ten. However, not only did they coincide in their appearance at the Bore, but Maidstone managed to take two very good flashlight photographs of Levvey and Nugget at the Bore with Joyce's cattle!

'After driving the cattle farther on, it was apparently decided that Nugget should return and dispose of Maidstone, and this he did.'

'I still don't see how it could last,' objected Newton. 'They must have been crazy.'

'Well,' Bony said, 'with the money involved, had it

gone on a little longer, Levvey could have got out of the country. And don't forget that there wasn't much to implicate Nugget. He could have stayed on the Fence long enough to allay suspicion and then quietly drifted on as so many of his type of worker do. In fact, as we've seen for ourselves, the thing about it was that the scheme jolly nearly worked.'

'Yes, I can follow all that,' said Newton. 'But how on earth did you get on to what was going on?'

'Well,' said Bony, 'it became obvious that Maidstone must have been at Bore Ten at the same time as the duffers and although he had used two flash bulbs, the film that he took was missing. It was really Joyce, however, who put me on the track when he recalled that Maidstone said he had known Levvey. Then there was the obvious friendship of Nugget and Levvey. Nugget was the only one who could have alerted the Quinambie blacks to attack me. The information about my movements could only have been passed on to the blacks by Nugget. Also it was very obvious that he had discussed me at length with Levvey. Levvey's story of having a job for me was much too pat. I was getting too close to the truth and this was one of these games in which, when once embarked upon, the odd extra murder didn't make any difference.'

'When you were talkin' to Wells along the Fence that day, I suppose you were arranging a rendezvous at Lake Frome Station?'

'That's right,' said Bony. 'But Wells got bogged on the way in, and but for the diversion created by the

Monster, bless him, I might not have been sitting drinking with you now.'

'Why on earth should the Monster behave like an ordinary animal for long periods and then suddenly go berserk?' asked Newton. 'He seemed all right whenever I saw him.'

'I've got a theory about that,' said Bony. 'It would not have been beyond Levvey and Nugget to catch and deliberately ill-treat him to make him sufficiently vicious to bolster up the legend. Don't forget it was always a native or half-caste he went for, first Luke, then Nugget. He was always nervous when Nugget was about, and if I had to pick the tormentor it would be Nugget. My Superintendent was a bit sore about him still roaming that country. I suppose you heard he got away?' Bony looked innocently at Newton.

Newton choked on his beer and started to speak, thought better of it, and drained his glass.

Bony refilled the glasses. 'And now,' he said, as he sat down again, 'there's one thing you'll be glad to hear. I never thought that I would get rid of the taste of the sand from that confounded Fence of yours and get the dryness, caused by that howling westerly wind, out of my throat. I now must admit that my throat is neither as dry, nor is the taste quite as bad, as when I first met you here today.'

Newton grinned, and raised his glass. 'A toast,' he said. 'To the finest Fence in the outback, coupled with the name of the Lake Frome Monster!'

# ARTHUR W. UPFIELD

## MASTERPIECES OF DETECTION

## NOW AVAILABLE IN ARKON PAPERBACKS

## THE DEVIL'S STEPS

Detective-Inspector Napoleon Bonaparte
leaves his familiar outback environment
for Melbourne and a nearby mountain
resort on a special assignment for
Military Intelligence.
Although out of his element among city
people, Bony displays his characteristic
skills to interpret some puzzling clues
and catch a murderer — providing the
ingredients for another fascinating Arthur
Upfield mystery.

# ARTHUR W. UPFIELD

## WINDS OF EVIL

When Detective-Inspector Napoleon
Bonaparte sets out to investigate two
bizarre murders at Wirragatta Station all
the odds are against him. The crimes
were committed a year before and the
scent is now cold, and any clues that
have survived have been confused by a
bumbling policeman.
As Bony follows the trail, he is first
threatened and then attacked by the
mysterious murderer. It's a case which
taxes his ingenuity to the limit.

## DEATH OF A SWAGMAN

"Our distinctive student of violence
arrives incognito at Merino, in western
New South Wales, and, as a first move,
provokes the local sergeant to lock him
up. The method in Bony's madness is
that while serving a semi-detention
sentence and being made to paint the
police station, he wears the best of all
disguises . . . Here again is a first-rate
Upfield mystery, made warm by humour,
by the background characters and his
portrayal of the natural background
scene."
— **The Age, Melbourne.**